LEGEND OF THE DEAD MEN'S GOLD

Ten years ago, the Helliton gang holed up in a stronghold with a stolen wagonload of gold. One year later, all of them were dead — fallen defending their hoard from other outlaws, and fighting amongst themselves. The last living gang member cursed the gold, saying that if he couldn't have it, nobody would. Or so the legend goes . . . Trip Kincaid had always been fascinated by the tale. His brother Oliver suspects it's the true reason behind his sudden disappearance — and is determined to find him . . .

Books by I. J. Parnham
in the Linford Western Library:

I. J. PARNHAM

LEGEND OF THE DEAD MEN'S GOLD

Complete and Unabridged

LINFORD
Leicester

First published in Great Britain in 2014 by
Robert Hale Limited
London

First Linford Edition
published 2016
by arrangement with
Robert Hale Limited
London

*A catalogue record for this book is available
from the British Library.*

ISBN 978–1–4448–2898–6

Published by
F. A. Thorpe (Publishing)
Anstey, Leicestershire

Set by Words & Graphics Ltd.
Anstey, Leicestershire
Printed and bound in Great Britain by
T. J. International Ltd., Padstow, Cornwall

This book is printed on acid-free paper

1

'It's been a long time,' Oliver Kincaid said, 'since you last came to Dirtwood, but I don't have any information for you.'

Newton Clay glanced around the nearly empty saloon room and shrugged.

'That's not important. This time *I* have information.'

Oliver nodded and placed a whiskey bottle on the bar. He poured Newton a generous measure, but when Newton fished in his pocket for money he shook his head.

'For a man with information the first drink is free.'

'I'm meeting someone here later.' Newton lowered his voice, even though the few customers in the Hunter's Moon weren't paying him any attention. 'Our discussion may touch upon the fate of this saloon's former owner, which is sure to interest a man who's prepared to provide free drinks all night.'

Oliver raised his hat to run fingers through his sparse hair.

'If I had a dollar for every customer who's tried to sell me details of what happened to my brother . . . '

'How much would you have?'

'About five hundred dollars.'

'Now that's a coincidence.' Newton swirled his drink. 'Because for five hundred dollars I'll tell you what happened to Trip.'

'If I had five hundred dollars I wouldn't be tending bar.'

'Four hundred?'

Oliver sighed. 'Do we have to waste time on this ritual? When you've had a few drinks you know you'll tell me everything for nothing.'

'Three hundred, then?' Newton frowned when Oliver shook his head. 'I'll whet your appetite with the name of a town for free: it's Helliton.'

'The place they call Hell Town?'

Oliver raised an eyebrow. 'It's said there's no way into that outlaw stronghold.'

'There isn't, except I'm meeting Santiago Pinchete. He plans to take over Helliton and he wants a town-tamer. So I thought I'd take his offer and your money; two hundred dollars, to be precise.'

'I tend bar.' Oliver tapped the whiskey bottle. 'I don't have two hundred dollars.'

Newton chuckled with a gleam in his eye that said the negotiation was closing in on the right price. Oliver merely topped up his glass before he moved to the other end of the bar but, as it turned out, Newton didn't try to continue their conversation.

For the next hour Newton nursed his glass while Oliver served his customers. Later two men he'd never seen before arrived individually.

One man took a glass of whiskey to a table, choosing a position where he could watch the door, while the other man joined Newton.

'I'm surprised you came,' Newton said after introducing Oliver to Gabriel Bigelow.

'I'm still looking for a way into Helliton,' Gabriel said. 'But I haven't changed my opinion that town-taming is a bad way to make money.'

'Having information is always the easiest way.' Newton gestured at Oliver. 'For instance, my old friend has promised to give me a hundred dollars to solve an old mystery.'

Oliver paused from cleaning glasses to shake his head while, from the corner of his eye, Gabriel considered the other newcomer, who was passing the time by flicking a gold eagle from hand to hand.

'You said Santiago hadn't made this offer to anyone else.'

'I didn't think he had.'

'Then who's the gunslinger?'

'That's Erebus Finch, twice as fast on the draw as a spooked rattler and twice as mean.'

Newton nodded before joining Gabriel in leaning on the bar in pensive silence.

It was approaching midnight and Oliver's regular customers were sloping away when a tall, stern man arrived. Erebus straightened up while Newton and Gabriel beckoned him on, confirming this man was Santiago Pinchete.

At the bar Santiago inspected his glass for marks before he let Oliver pour him a whiskey. He led Newton and Gabriel to Erebus's table where he considered the last straggler.

Newton caught Oliver's eye and, getting his meaning, Oliver rounded this man up and directed him to the door. This late in the evening he had difficulty in walking and so by the time Oliver had cleared out the room the meeting was under way.

While Santiago outlined his offer quietly Oliver, despite claiming the meeting didn't interest him, stood by the table holding a whiskey bottle.

Although he couldn't hear what Santiago was saying Newton noted, with a sly smile, his attempt to eavesdrop.

Oliver had accepted he wouldn't hear anything interesting and he was gravitating back to the bar when Gabriel scraped back his chair and stood up.

'I've heard enough of this madness,' he declared. 'Any man who tries to tame Helliton won't survive to enjoy his first sundown.'

Gabriel glanced at Newton, who shrugged, while Santiago spread his hands, showing he wouldn't try to talk him round. So while shaking his head Gabriel made for the door.

Santiago waited until he'd gone before he gestured for Oliver to top up their glasses.

'So that leaves me to choose between you two,' he said as Oliver poured three full whiskey glasses. 'I hope whichever one of you I pick will enjoy more than one sundown.'

'That'll depend,' Newton said, 'on

how Helliton reacts to its first town-tamer.'

'They'll react badly. I'm looking for the fourth town-tamer.'

Newton winced and Erebus tipped back his hat, this being the most animated reaction that Oliver had seen him make.

'What happened to the first three?' Oliver asked.

He winced after contributing to the discussion for the first time, and sure enough Santiago considered him with a cold look while leaning back in his chair.

'That's of no interest to a bartender.'

'But,' Newton said, interrupting presumably to reduce Oliver's embarrassment, 'it's a good question.'

Santiago nodded and bade Oliver to stay and hear the answer.

'I guess an inquisitive bartender should know. The first was gunned down from four different directions before his first sundown. The second took the precaution of staying in the office I'd given him. Two days later I found him slumped over his desk, having been shot in the back.'

'And the third?' Newton asked.

'He killed the second, so I decided I needed a new man from out of town, which brings me back to the question of which one of you do I choose.'

Santiago looked from one man to the other while Newton considered Erebus, his raised eyebrows inviting him to speak for the first time. Erebus still took several moments to respond.

'Choose,' he said, his voice almost too low for Oliver to hear him, 'wisely.'

'I'm a ruthless man,' Newton said. He picked up his glass and raised it in salute to his rival. 'Are you?'

Erebus opened his hand, revealing the eagle he'd been tossing earlier. He flicked the coin and caught it.

Erebus nodded, as if he approved of the result although he hadn't looked at the coin. Then, with a thin smile on his lips, he moved to take his glass with his left hand.

The action made Oliver uneasy. By the time he'd identified his concern and Erebus, while tossing the coin, had shown himself to be right-handed, it was too late.

Erebus used his motion of leaning forward to disguise his slipping his hand down to his holster. Then he ripped his six-shooter out and, before anyone could move, in a fluid motion he fired.

His gunshot sliced into Newton's chest, making Newton throw his head back in shock, his expression being one of surprise tinged with pain. His gaze sought out Oliver before he slid from his chair and slumped over in an ungainly heap on the floor.

'I am,' Erebus said. He turned to Santiago.

Santiago raised himself to consider Newton's form before tearing his gaze away.

'I believe,' he murmured, 'I've found the right man.'

Luckily, Santiago then ignored Oliver

while Erebus merely cast him a disdainful glance that both warned him to stay back and acknowledged that he was only a bartender. As both men left the table and walked to the door, Oliver dropped to his knees and rolled Newton over on to his back.

'I guess,' Newton breathed with his eyes pained and narrowed, 'fifty dollars is out of the question?'

'I'll pay you whatever you want, but the information can wait until I can get you — '

'Too late,' Newton said through gritted teeth. He grabbed Oliver's arm. 'You can have everything I know about Trip for nothing. Find the queen of hearts.'

Oliver waited for more, but Newton's hand was loosening its grip. Oliver shook his shoulders.

'What does that mean? How does that . . . ?'

He trailed off as Newton's hand slipped away from his arm and landed on the floor with a thud.

The newcomer held a drawn gun and sported a fierce scowl, but Vaughan Price still smiled broadly.

'I assume you'd like a fast horse,' he said while spreading his hands and inviting the man into the stable. 'And you're in luck, as I have plenty.'

'You assumed wrong,' the man said. He walked towards Vaughan. 'I want information.'

Vaughan rubbed his hands. 'I might have that too.'

The man stomped to a halt and rubbed his bristled jaw.

'Then tell me about Ballard Swift.'

'Ah.' Vaughan took an involuntary pace backwards. 'I don't know much about him.'

'You sure knew plenty when you spilled your guts to the bounty hunter Gabriel Bigelow.' The man raised an eyebrow, inviting a response, but Vaughan's mouth had gone dry. 'Last month Gabriel tracked Ballard down

11

and Ballard got a bellyful of lead. It took him two days to die.'

Vaughan gulped, but the action failed to moisten his throat.

'Did you know Ballard well?'

'I'm Tobias Swift.' The newcomer squared up to Vaughan, grabbed his collar and hoisted him up on tiptoes. Cold metal jabbed into the underside of Vaughan's jaw. 'And I'm here to give you a choice.'

'What choice?' Vaughan bleated, glancing down at the gun.

Tobias walked Vaughan backwards. 'It's a simple one: I can make this either real quick or real slow.'

'There has to be another way.' Vaughan waved his arms as he struggled to keep his balance. 'I . . . I . . . I told Gabriel nothing other than I sold Ballard a horse, and he hadn't even come to Prudence about Ballard.'

'Stop babbling and choose.' Tobias jabbed the gun deep into Vaughan's skin, making him raise his chin.

'I don't want to choose. I must have

something you want.' Vaughan met Tobias's eye. He saw no hope of a reprieve in the man's cold gaze, but with Tobias taking his time over enacting his revenge, he thought quickly and then opted for his best chance. 'Have you heard of the legend of the dead men's gold?'

With an angry snarl Tobias threw Vaughan backwards, making him go clattering into the side of a stall before he broke through the wood and went sprawling on his back.

'Ballard got shot up because of your tales.' Tobias came round the end of the stall and trained his gun on Vaughan's stomach. 'So I sure don't want to hear no stories about cursed gold.'

'It's not a story. That's what Gabriel Bigelow came to see me about.' Vaughan raised his hands in a beseeching gesture. 'I know the secret of the gold!'

Tobias sneered. 'The legend says that only dead men find the gold.'

Vaughan noted that Tobias had

lowered his gun slightly, so, while he still had a chance to talk his way out of his predicament, he got up on to his knees and offered a smile.

'In my current situation that don't concern me.'

Tobias narrowed his eyes, but when Vaughan said no more, he returned the smile.

'Show me the gold,' he said, 'and you'll get to prove the legend wrong.'

2

'Who was he?' Doctor Tweedmouth asked after confirming Newton's demise.

'I don't know,' Oliver said, not meeting Tweedmouth's eye. 'He said he was passing through and he was a friendly enough customer, but clearly he and the other man had a problem with each other.'

'And I assume you don't know who the other man was either?'

'You know me. I don't ask no questions.'

'I'll be sure to tell that to any lawman who takes an interest.'

Tweedmouth considered Oliver with a raised eyebrow, inviting him to offer a better explanation, but Oliver turned away and walked out of the surgery. It was past midnight and Santiago and Erebus had already left town, presumably on their way to Helliton.

As Oliver wandered past quiet buildings he pondered on what Newton's last words had meant. So as he went into his saloon he had his head lowered and it took him several moments to register that he had customers.

When he noticed the four men who were loitering around the saloon room with surly gleams in their eyes, he stopped two paces in from the doorway.

'I'm closed,' he said.

'You look open to me,' the man at the bar said. He had his back to him and he was leaning over his glass of whiskey.

Oliver put on a fixed, good-host smile and walked behind the bar to face him.

'It's been a long day, but enjoy your drinks before you leave.'

Oliver raised an eyebrow, inviting the man to offer a name, and he admitted to being Rex Amney, a name that meant nothing to Oliver, before gulping his drink.

'I assume that means you've had

plenty of visitors tonight?' Rex smiled slyly and looked at the dark stain in the corner where Newton had breathed his last.

'It's not been a trouble-free night.'

This non-committal answer made Rex nod, and the other men took this as their cue to move closer. Sure enough, when the first man reached the bar, Rex swirled round, his hand rising to grab Oliver's collar.

Oliver jerked aside and Rex's hand closed on air.

'You move quickly for a fat bar-tender.'

'You ask too many questions for a customer.'

Rex snarled as he scooped up his whiskey glass and hurled it at Oliver. The whiskey sprayed out of the glass and splashed into Oliver's face.

With his eyes burning, Oliver backed away and by the time he'd shaken the liquor from his eyes Rex had rolled over the bar. Then, while moving forward, he thudded a low punch into Oliver's rounded belly, which made him groan and fold over.

The moment Oliver straightened Rex ran him at the bar, making Oliver belly-up to the bar and tumble over it. He landed on the floor on his side, from where, as fast as he was able, he got to his feet, but already two men had closed in on him.

They grabbed one arm apiece and shoved him backwards to pin him against the bar. They held him until Rex joined them. He considered Oliver with a smirk on his face.

'Why did Santiago come here?' Rex asked.

'He met Erebus Finch,' Oliver said, starting with the simplest part of tonight's events.

Rex flinched, while the men holding Oliver tensed before they looked at Rex for instructions. Rex took his time in replying, his eyes glazing as he digested information that had clearly troubled him.

When he got over his surprise, with

an angry grunt he slapped Oliver's cheek backhanded, sending him leaning backwards over the bar. When Oliver righted himself, Rex delivered a fierce two-fisted blow that settled deep into his substantial stomach.

Only the men holding him upright ensured he didn't crumple to his knees. He still lowered his head, which let Rex slap the back of his neck with a double-handed blow that tore him away from the men holding him.

He went sprawling on the floor where he lay on his chest, gasping for air while willing the pain in his stomach and neck to recede. When he'd regained enough of his senses to feel confident that he could stand up, he raised his head, shaking it, only to see Rex's boot swinging towards his face.

He tried to swerve away from the foot, but he was too slow to avoid a stinging kick to the jaw that sent him rolling along until he fetched up against the base of the bar.

He lay grunting in pain and tasting

blood, and he must have blacked out, as he sensed that the men were no longer standing around him. He flitted in and out of consciousness while a disjointed conversation ensued, the voices sounding fuzzy and seemingly coming from a distance.

He couldn't concentrate on what was being discussed, although he heard them talking about Erebus Finch and Santiago Pinchete before the murmured conversation coalesced into a low and soothing buzzing sound.

Harsh brightness and warmth dragged him back to consciousness, making him think it was morning. He could no longer hear the conversation and he didn't sense that anyone was close by, so he stretched out, giving himself time to regain his strength.

Liquid dripped on his outstretched hand, the shock made him draw the hand away. The back of his hand still felt odd and it wasn't until a cloying taste in his throat made him cough that he realized the liquid had been hot and that it had scalded him.

He coughed hard and raised his head. Now he saw that it was still night-time and the light and heat came from a fire that had taken hold of an upturned table. He raised his head higher and saw the fire had spread to other tables, chairs, the wall. Worst of all, flames were skittering across the floor towards him.

Despite the danger, Oliver struggled to concentrate on the approaching flames. He must have lost consciousness again as the next thing he knew the flames were skating along to cut off his escape route to the door. As his right side was being roasted, he put his left hand to the bar and, with every breath a struggle, he drew himself up to his knees.

He rested his cheek against the bar enjoying the relatively cooler temperature of the wood before he slapped his hands on the top to draw himself up. Heat flashed across his fingers making him cringe away and he went crashing down on his back.

Flames now surrounded him, baking him from all sides, but although the eye-watering heat and the dazzling light meant he had to move or die, he closed his eyes.

He lay on his back breathing shallowly with his arms crossed and resting on his chest, a posture that strangely felt right although equally strangely, someone started speaking urgently near by.

Oliver couldn't discern the words, so he didn't respond until a heavy cloth was slapped across his shins. He murmured in complaint as he was turned over and slapped on the back. Then firm hands grabbed his arms.

Vaguely he shooed the man away, but the man didn't heed him and he was dragged face down across the saloon floor. The heat intensified and the man shouted a complaint about his weight, but then the temperature dropped and it became dark.

Oliver accepted he'd been dragged

outside as grit was now beneath him. Then his rescuer took his arms and drew him to his feet.

Oliver tried to tell the man to leave him alone, but that made him cough uncontrollably, and he couldn't stop himself being led away until he was swung round and set down against a wall.

His vision was blurred, but he could see a burning building ahead. As he watched the flames lick at the windows and consume the walls, only slowly did his groggy state recede and let him accept he had been dragged out of that building.

Several seconds passed before he realized the building was the Hunter's Moon. He groaned and closed his eyes.

* * *

'How do you feel?' Doctor Tweedmouth said, peering down at him.

'My legs are sore and my throat's raw,' Oliver croaked. He raised himself slightly from the table, but then thought better of moving and flopped back down on his back. 'The worst thing is my head feels like it's going to split in two, but all that won't feel so painful if you tell me my saloon was saved.'

'I can't tell you that.' Tweedmouth pointed at the man loitering in the doorway of his surgery. 'But thanks to him, you're alive.'

'Obliged for what . . . ' Oliver trailed off when his saviour moved closer to reveal that he was Gabriel Bigelow, the man who had left the meeting with Santiago Pinchete.

'I heard there'd been a shooting,' Gabriel said. 'So I came back to find out what had happened, only to see your saloon burning down.'

'It's lucky for me that you did, and it's lucky for you that you left that meeting.' Oliver lowered his voice so that Tweedmouth wouldn't hear him. 'Erebus Finch gunned down Newton Clay in cold blood.'

Gabriel nodded, his expression

impassive. Then he turned to leave, so Oliver clambered off the doctor's table.

He ignored Tweedmouth's demand that he rest up until he was stronger and, with his head bowed and adopting a shuffling gait, he followed Gabriel out of the surgery.

'Don't feel obligated to me,' Gabriel said. 'I just happened to be in a position to help you and I only did what anyone else would do.'

'Except you're the only man who did help me.' Oliver broke off to cough and clear his lungs of the stench of smoke. 'I assume as you're looking for a way into Hell Town and Newton got shot up, you'll follow Erebus?'

Gabriel glanced at the smouldering saloon.

'That's no concern of yours.'

'So do you know Rex Amney? Or Trip Kincaid?' Oliver received uncommitted grunts. 'Then how do you know Newton?'

'I don't have to answer your questions.'

'You don't, but Newton wanted to tell me something, except he died before he said anything that made sense. Perhaps you can fill in the blanks.'

Gabriel considered him, his furrowed brow showing he was wondering if he should confide in him before, with a nod, he spoke up.

'Newton went after the outlaw Ballard Swift, but I found him first. As we both followed the same trail and Santiago's offer enticed him, it's likely Newton heard the same intriguing tale I did.'

'About what?'

'About the legend of the dead men's gold,' Gabriel said levelly.

Oliver snorted a laugh, but when Gabriel faced him with his jaw set firm, he shook his head sadly.

'If I had a dollar for every man who came into my saloon with information about that story . . . ' Oliver waited, but

Gabriel didn't prompt him. 'I'd have retired years ago.'

'Maybe so, but there's a truth behind the legend.'

'The legend says the last member of the Helliton gang cursed the gold, saying if he couldn't have it, nobody would. Now the bones of all the men who have died trying to get their hands on the gold lie strewn around it, so nobody would want to know the truth.'

'I'm not interested in tall tales about curses and bones. All that interests me is the facts,' stated Gabriel.

'Which are?'

'Ten years ago the Helliton gang were the first outlaws to hole up in the stronghold. They were blamed for every unexplained crime within five hundred miles, so nobody knows the full extent of their crimes, but many people reckoned they holed up because they'd stolen a wagonload of gold. A year later, when they'd all died from fighting off other outlaws and from fighting amongst themselves, nobody could find the gold.'

'So surely the one place the gold can't be is in Hell Town?'

'The information I gathered says otherwise.'

Oliver frowned. 'Does my brother Trip feature in this information? Because the legend fascinated him too and Newton said he went to Hell Town.'

'No, and I've told you everything I'm prepared to reveal. I'll leave you to your business now.'

'Except I have no business now.' Oliver turned to the wreckage. 'I used to tend bar. I don't no more.'

3

Sunup found Oliver searching through the remnants of the Hunter's Moon for anything that was worth saving.

He found little to salvage. So, by late morning he sat on a mound behind the building with his few possessions spread out around him.

He had the handful of dollars he'd been carrying when Rex Amney had torched the building, and a change of clothes, although as he was still wearing the singed clothes from last night that didn't cheer him.

As everything else had been burnt to a crisp, he couldn't help but dwell on the fate of his younger brother, and the former owner of what had once been a prosperous business.

Oliver had tended bar for the charismatic Trip while the customers had come to hear Trip's tales about his colourful exploits, resulting in the saloon being full every night. Oliver had heard Trip's tall tales many times and he hadn't believed them, until one of the stories had been proved true.

Trip had claimed he'd won something valuable in a high-stakes poker game, but afterwards the previous owner had decided the game was crooked and he'd wanted it back.

Unlike with his other tales, Trip had been nervous and he had told only Oliver. He'd also provided only sparse details while refusing Oliver's request for him to explain what he'd won and who he'd won it from.

This suggested that this time he had told the truth. Oliver had recommended that Trip should lie low, and so they had hatched a plan.

While Oliver looked after the saloon Trip would make himself scarce. If anyone came looking for him Oliver would say that he didn't know where he had gone, which was true. Then, after a suitable period Trip would return.

Ominously Trip made the typically generous offer that if he didn't return within a year, Oliver should conclude his nemesis had found him and the saloon would become Oliver's. As it had turned out, nobody had sought Trip out, and he was so successful at making himself scarce that nobody knew where he had gone.

After a year Oliver had, with a heavy heart, deemed the saloon to be his, but sadly it had already become clear that he wasn't as successful a saloon owner as Trip had been.

Trip had been an animated host while Oliver was a quiet man who ran a quiet establishment. So the Silver Star, the only other saloon in town, had prospered while his custom had dropped off.

'You're looking thoughtful.'

Oliver flinched and it took him several moments to shake off his reverie and note that Doctor Tweedmouth had come to see him.

'I am,' he said, gesturing at the

wreckage. 'But then again, everything I had has been taken away.'

'The man who died last night could claim he'd lost everything.'

Oliver conceded Tweedmouth's point with a nod and made his way to the heap of objects he'd rescued. He returned with a half-burnt saloon sign on which only the word 'Moon' had survived.

'Are you saying I should stop feeling sorry for myself and build another saloon where I can hang this sign outside?'

'I wasn't, but if that's what you want to do, then do it.'

Oliver turned the sign round to consider it.

'I guess I don't have no choice. The only thing I know how to do is to tend bar, and Dirtwood needs two saloons.' Oliver looked at Tweedmouth. 'Even if I attracted your custom only rarely.'

Tweedmouth shrugged. 'When Trip ran the saloon, I used to come in most nights.'

Tweedmouth winced, presumably after realizing that his unsubtle comment was the last thing Oliver needed to hear, but it made Oliver smile ruefully.

'You weren't the only one, so perhaps I should confront my limitations. I'm just a bartender. I can serve drinks, mop up, lend a sympathetic ear, but I was never the right man to own a saloon. Trip was.'

'Trip's long gone.'

'So they say.'

Oliver hefted the saloon sign. Then he hurled it into the middle of the burnt timber.

A puff of ash and smoke rose up, but by the time it had dissipated, Oliver was striding away down the main drag. An hour later he rode out of town, his destination Helliton.

★ ★ ★

'We should wait until it's dark,' Vaughan Price said.

'If we do that,' Tobias Swift replied,

'we won't be able to see what we're doing.'

Then Tobias tripped and cursed, rendering Vaughan's intended retort unnecessary. Instead, he shuffled the coil of rope into a position where his arms weren't constrained before he embarked on the treacherous climb.

He hadn't let his unwelcome colleague know he wasn't optimistic about their chances of getting into Helliton. Since they had left Prudence two days ago he had appeared confident about the information he had been given, but that didn't make their task any easier.

Everyone knew it was impossible to sneak into Helliton, as that was the reason the Helliton gang had holed up here in the first place and why it had defied all attempts to flush anyone out.

Helliton was in a box canyon, which had only one narrow mouth. That entrance was always guarded, ensuring that nobody who wasn't welcome gained access, or at least that was the accepted story, as several years ago

Vaughan had heard a rumour about another secret way in.

He had accepted the rumour without interest, as he'd had no desire to go to Helliton. That attitude hadn't changed when he'd heard a second rumour that the dead men's gold was still in Helliton.

Now he had no choice but to hope both rumours had substance.

Promisingly, the first rumour appeared valid as the start of the climb lay behind two unremarkable boulders that suggested that the second way in could have remained secret.

The route up the side of the steep ridge appeared climbable with care. So Vaughan put a hand on a ledge and drew himself up while Tobias fell in behind him.

They moved on. As the ascent was sheer and gloom was gathering Vaughan climbed as quickly as he dared, seizing his first opportunity to put distance between himself and Tobias. He didn't help him by pointing out difficult parts of the climb, in the hope that Tobias would stumble and fall, but whenever Vaughan glanced down Tobias was clambering up only a few feet below him.

He judged he'd ascended for a hundred feet when the climb became less sheer. Tobias drew alongside and on hands and knees they clambered over rocks until they reached the summit.

Tobias hooted with delight, but his joy was short-lived as once they'd crested the high point, a steeper summit was ahead, the craggy rocks proving why this outlaw stronghold was deemed to be impenetrable.

'Which way?' Tobias asked.

Vaughan's information about the secret path had only involved locating the two boulders, but as no further information had been provided, he assumed the route would present itself. So with apparent confidence he set off in the lead and after a dozen paces he found a gap between rocks that curved to the right while getting ever higher.

At first they made good progress, but by the time they'd covered half the distance to the highest point, the closeness of the surrounding rocks made the darkness deepen quickly and he stumbled over most paces.

He stopped and turned. Tobias's form was just a dark outline in the night with only his eyes reflecting stray light.

'It's now too dark to see where we're going,' Vaughan said. 'We have to hole up.'

'You wanted to wait for darkness,' Tobias muttered. He raised his hat to scratch his head. 'Does this mean you're lost?'

'I know which way to go, but I hadn't realized it'd be this treacherous in the dark.'

Tobias shoved Vaughan on. 'That's why you're leading.'

While Tobias laughed, Vaughan clambered on, feeling his way forward while straining his eyes to catch any light. After two dozen paces, this appeared to work as he saw a lighter patch ahead.

The lightness didn't help him move any easier and he slowed so much that Tobias was at his heels. He wondered if his vision was playing tricks on him, but the lighter patch expanded until he discerned that he was heading into a gap, letting him see the night sky ahead.

Dark rocks towered above him, but he presumed they wouldn't have to scale the highest peak. Confident now that he'd found the secret path he speeded up and, as he saw more of the night sky, diffused light, presumably from the town, cast a glow and made the going easier.

The slope petered out, followed by a flat stretch and then he went downwards. Vaughan craned his neck trying to work out the lie of the land ahead as behind him Tobias muttered something.

Vaughan ignored him and he strode along more assuredly only for him to miss his footing and pitch forward. In a sudden alarming moment he saw lights below and he realized he'd reached the edge of the canyon faster than he'd expected, but by then he was struggling for balance.

With his arms wheeling he teetered on the lip of a bone-snapping drop down to the rocks below, but inexorably he tipped forward. He felt as if he were leaning forward so far that his head was level with his knees when Tobias's hand closed around his wrist.

He sighed with relief as Tobias dragged him away from the edge. Then he clutched a boulder while he willed his heart to stop hammering.

After his brush with death, he would have gladly stayed there and let Tobias take the lead, but Tobias prised him away from the rock and removed the coil of rope from his shoulder.

With his eyes now accustomed to the gloom, he could see the edge and so he peered down. The drop was sheer and the rock was smooth, but that was one of the reasons why he'd brought rope.

While Tobias secured a noose around a boulder, he took deep breaths to regain his confidence. Even so, he didn't look down as he clambered over the edge. Then, leaning back with his feet braced against the rock, he effectively walked downwards.

Tobias disappeared from view and the featureless rock meant he couldn't work out how far he descended. When cramps tightened his arms he looked down and to his relief saw that he was five feet off the ground.

Feeling more hopeful than at any time since leaving Prudence, he swung down to the ground and tugged the rope to signal his success. Shuffling sounded as Tobias prepared to follow him down, so he moved away from the rope into the shadows.

When he was far enough away to avoid Tobias's body if he were to fall, he stopped. He couldn't see him, but he still heard shuffling and it became more frantic, suggesting Tobias was in trouble.

As Vaughan smiled a crunch sounded, alerting him a moment before a man stepped up behind him. An arm wrapped around his neck while a blunt object jabbed into his back.

A gunshot tore out high above him. Tobias shouted before rapid gunfire blasted as he fought for his life.

A prolonged cry of terror sounded. It came closer until Tobias slammed down to the ground with a sickening crunch. Tobias didn't move, and though Vaughan strained his neck he couldn't see his captor.

'You didn't believe the rumours,' the man said in his ear, 'of there being a secret way in here, did you?'

4

Two days after leaving Dirtwood, Oliver's old friend Bill Ruben, who tended bar for the Liberty saloon in Prudence, reported that Rex Amney had passed through earlier that day.

The news that Erebus and Santiago were a day ahead and moving quickly had made Rex loiter before he sloped out of town. Like Rex, the news also made Oliver loiter and he settled down at the end of the bar for a meal, but an hour of pondering didn't change his plans.

He was heading to Helliton to find out what had happened to Trip. Revenge against Rex for burning down his saloon and against Erebus for killing Newton would remain wishful fancy.

He was podgy, unfit, and at his age the hair on his head was thinner than the hair on his arms. Worse, he was unarmed and he'd never owned, or for that matter ever fired, a six-shooter in his life.

'I'm no gunslinger,' he said to himself with a sigh, 'I'm just a bartender.'

'That's not a problem,' Bill said, making Oliver frown on realizing he'd spoken his thoughts aloud.

'It is when your destination is Hell Town. Apparently, Trip fetched up there.'

'If he did, a man like you won't prove it. Nobody gets into Hell Town without a good reason, such as evading the law, having stolen goods to sell, or having more money than sense.'

'I know that, but I'll have to see it for myself.'

'There's a rumour our ostler Vaughan Price went there. He hasn't returned and I don't want to lose another friend.' Bill gestured at the busy saloon room. 'But I could use a good worker.'

'Obliged for the offer, but Trip is the only man I want to work for.'

With that determined statement

renewing his sense of purpose, Oliver bade Bill goodbye and left town. As he rode along he tried to devise a plan that was more sophisticated than riding to Helliton and hoping to find a way in.

His mind stayed blank, but when the sun grew large and red, making him look for a place to rest up for the night, he saw a campfire glow coming from behind a mound. As he assumed this was Rex Amney, he rode past the mound and doubled back along lower ground.

He dismounted and clambered to the top where, on his chest, he crawled along. Fifty yards below sat Rex, who was chatting and displaying no sign that he'd seen him, so Oliver relaxed and for the next hour, as the light level dropped, he watched him.

He decided Rex couldn't get away with what he'd done. Stealing any valuables Rex had would be appropriate retribution and he figured that, when he reached Helliton, the experience would be useful.

The fire was the only light illuminating the mound as he got up on his haunches and noted several covering boulders, but a hand slapped across his mouth and drew him backwards. By the time he realized someone had sneaked up on him, he could only struggle ineffectually as he was dragged away.

Halfway down the other side of the mound he was turned round. The firelight didn't reach this far and he could see only his captor's dark form.

'Dragging you away from trouble,' this man said, 'is becoming a habit.'

When Oliver recognized the voice, he relaxed and uttered a low grunt that made Gabriel Bigelow remove his hand.

'As you're going after the dead men's gold,' Oliver said hopefully, 'it seems we're heading in the same direction.'

Gabriel directed Oliver to quieten. Then they headed down the mound.

'I'm not wasting my time saving your butt,' Gabriel said when they were far enough away from the campsite to talk freely.

'Except back there you didn't save me. I knew what I was doing and I was in no danger.'

'You had no idea what you were doing and you was in a heap of danger. Only three men were beside the fire while the fourth man was lying in wait for anyone who might sneak up on them.'

Oliver opened his mouth to rebut the claim, but then with a sigh he thought better of it.

'I hadn't seen that.' He shrugged. 'I'm new at this sort of thing.'

'Then what in tarnation are you doing out here?'

Oliver gestured back east. 'I lost a friend and my saloon, and my brother was last seen in Hell Town.'

'I know that. My question still stands.'

Oliver grunted with irritation. 'From what I've heard, aside from outlaws the only people who get into Hell Town have more money than sense. I don't know if you have money, but as you believe a tall tale about cursed gold, it's clear you don't have no sense.'

Gabriel sighed. 'Either way, I have a better chance of getting in than you do.'

Oliver set his hands on his hips. 'Because I'm just a bartender?'

Gabriel considered him while nodding.

'Perhaps,' he mused, 'a bartender is just the man I need to get in, after all.'

★   ★   ★

'Rex is far behind us,' Oliver said after they'd been riding for an hour. 'We can travel slower.'

'I'm not worried about him,' Gabriel said. 'Erebus and Santiago will have reached Helliton by now and I want to follow them in before sundown.'

'How do you know that?'

Gabriel shot him an aggrieved look that said he shouldn't question his abilities again; then he rode on at a brisk trot. Oliver didn't mind him not being forthcoming, as his chances of getting into Helliton had improved and he was safer.

As his disdain for Gabriel's mission and his lack of suitability for his own mission had tried Gabriel's patience, last night he had stayed silent and today he avoided chatter. By the time the sun was halfway down to the horizon this had appeared to thaw Gabriel's stern attitude as, when he stopped on a high point, Gabriel spoke without contempt.

'Helliton,' he said indicating the barren terrain ahead.

Oliver considered the blind valleys and crags splayed out for as far as he could see without detecting any sign of habitation.

'I don't see nothing,' he said.

'Which is why it exists.' Gabriel pointed at a gap between two unremarkable pinnacles of rock two miles away. 'It lies beyond that gap. Nobody gets close unseen and for ten years it's defied every attempt to flush anyone out, except that now Santiago has hired Erebus to tame this outlaw stronghold.'

Oliver looked beyond the pinnacles, trying to imagine the town, but with only rock being visible, he couldn't work out the settlement's likely extent.

'I can see how Hell Town got its reputation, but not why anyone would want to tame this place.'

'It's become a victim of its own success and Santiago has become wealthier than most. He doesn't care about the town, only about protecting his own gains at the end of a gun.'

Oliver frowned. 'I saw that in Dirtwood.'

'Yet you still came. That took guts.'

Oliver slapped his stomach. 'Nobody can ever doubt I've got guts.'

Gabriel laughed. 'But now you know what awaits us, you can still turn back. You might escape the people who are watching us.'

Oliver looked around. 'I haven't seen nobody.'

'Neither have I, but I always worry about the men I can't see, not the ones I can.'

Gabriel's stern expression made Oliver give a worried shake of the head that was more of a shiver than a denial.

'I've come this far. And apparently you think that as I'm a bartender, that'll somehow get us in.'

This reminder of last night's cryptic comment made Gabriel frown.

'Helliton doesn't need another gun, but like any town it provides entertainment and liquor, so it might welcome someone who can tend bar.'

Although this plan sounded no more likely to succeed than Oliver's own vague plans, he nodded. So, at a cautious pace, they moved to lower ground and on to the mouth of the canyon.

Gabriel's warning made Oliver look around for trouble while the back of his neck tingled with a feeling that he was being watched, but they closed on their destination without incident.

Even so, Oliver's heart thudded with mounting trepidation, making him question his reason for undertaking this foolhardy mission. A part of him even hoped they'd get sent on their way so he could at least always tell himself he'd tried and failed.

'What do you want me to do?' he asked when the entrance was a hundred yards ahead.

'Stay quiet. And stop being nervous.'

'I can do one of those.'

'But clearly not very well.'

Oliver snorted a laugh before he took the hint and rode silently. He slipped in behind Gabriel and, when they reached the entrance, he saw a shadow move.

'Ahead and up there,' he called, unable to stop himself speaking.

Gabriel grunted in affirmation, his tense tone suggesting this was the first movement he'd seen too.

A man clambered down to meet them, moving leisurely. Although he wouldn't reach them in time to bar their way, Gabriel stopped thirty yards away from the guard, presumably so they could beat a hasty retreat if this encounter turned bad.

Oliver drew alongside Gabriel and planned the route away, but the open ground made him imagine a scrambling escape while gunmen took pot shots at his back. When the guard stopped behind a boulder fifteen feet from the ground with only his head visible, Gabriel spoke up.

'I'm Gabriel Bigelow,' he called. 'My friend's a bartender looking for work.'

The guard looked across the entrance. A minute passed until an unseen signal, presumably, made him nod.

'Enter,' he said.

Oliver had convinced himself they wouldn't gain entrance and so when he had got over his surprise, he looked at Gabriel for guidance. Gabriel winked and at a walking pace they moved on.

With every pace Oliver expected the guard to reveal his true intent and for gunfire to hammer down at them, but they passed him without challenge.

A hundred yards ahead the entrance narrowed to a ravine with room for only two riders to ride together. Oliver had to grip the reins tightly to stop him hurrying out of the guard's sight. When they were halfway to relative safety, he cautiously looked over his shoulder.

'Don't look back,' Gabriel snapped. 'We're not safe yet.'

'But it's looking promising. Clearly Hell Town must be in desperate need of a bartender.'

Gabriel smiled and despite Oliver's resolution to remain calm, with the ravine thirty yards ahead he speeded up. He rode inside at a trot, although as the ravine swung to the right he had to slow down.

Glancing at the sheer rock that rose for 200 feet on either side, he rode on for several minutes. The snaking route confirmed that this place could be defended easily, but it also increased his trepidation about what awaited him.

When the ravine opened up to reveal the canyon, Oliver stopped to wait for Gabriel, while noting that it was wider in the middle with a blunt end, sheer sides and with a flat bottom. It provided enough space for two rows of buildings with a main drag facing the ravine.

Some buildings were close to the canyon sides; and most were crude clapboard constructions with those to the right being as flimsy as tents. On the left and further away the buildings were more substantial; the most impressive structure faced them, at the end of the canyon.

The only people visible were a group sitting on a wall around a circular stone well, which stood in the middle of town. These men glanced at them briefly before looking in the opposite direction, which made Gabriel and Oliver shrug before they moved on at a slow pace.

'I don't know what they're looking at,' Gabriel said when they reached the first buildings, 'but they're not interested in us, so we should take advantage and get under cover.'

Gabriel pointed at the large building at the end of the canyon. Oliver noted it was a saloon and, as it was the only two-storey building in town, he hoped it would offer rooms.

As they rode past the well, from the corner of his eye Oliver watched the people until he could no longer see them. Then he watched the buildings, feeling sure their good fortune couldn't last: that someone would come out to confront them.

They were halfway between the well and the saloon when, as if responding to an unseen signal, dozens of people spilled outside. This encouraged the men who had been loitering around the well to move purposefully, but Oliver's worst fears were not realized as the men moved away from the well and turned to the saloon.

'We've arrived either at the best time or the worst,' Oliver said, 'as something is about to happen.'

'Don't stop,' Gabriel said. 'Don't look back again, and don't get involved.'

Before Oliver could reply the saloon

doors flew open and a man came barrelling out, his speed suggesting that a firm kick had propelled him. He hit the ground on his side and rolled over twice before he fetched up on his back.

He shook himself and moved to get up, but then he saw the boisterous crowd, who shouted at him, revealing that his name was Jacques Herzog. He fled past the corner of the building next to the saloon, but a few moments later he returned, looking back over his shoulder.

When he looked forward he skidded to a halt. Then he rocked from foot to foot in indecision.

The developing situation made Gabriel and Oliver speed up. At a canter the two men rode around the corner of the next building, letting Oliver see that people were approaching from either side.

One way led to a corral and stable constructed against the canyon side while in the other direction stood the wreckage of a burnt-out building. The charred timbers looked undisturbed, suggesting that the fire was recent; it put Oliver in mind of the fate of his own saloon.

Fewer people were there, so Jacques hurried in that direction, but this made the approaching mob speed up and three men tried to intercept him. Within moments the scene became chaotic with people hurrying from all directions as they sought to cut off Jacques no matter in which direction he ran.

A gunshot blasted, which encouraged other men to hammer lead into the ground in front of their quarry. Jacques doubled back until another burst of gunfire made him skid to a halt and try yet another direction in which to flee.

As the shooting created a lively atmosphere, with people whooping and hollering, Oliver caught Gabriel's attention.

'We have to do something,' he said.

'We will,' Gabriel replied. 'We'll take our horses to the stable. Then we'll stay out of sight.'

A dozen men had now formed a loose circle around Jacques so reluctantly, Oliver had to agree. He hurried after Gabriel, who rode into the stable without looking back.

Oliver followed him in, but while Gabriel spoke to the ostler, who identified himself as Yohann Johanson, he dismounted and looked outside. Jacques was now standing alone, the tormentors who had trapped him spreading out.

The reason for their behaviour became apparent when Erebus Finch emerged from the saloon, holding a six-shooter drawn and pointing downwards. When Erebus stomped to a halt, Jacques considered him with horror etched into his drawn features. Then he took to his heels and sprinted down the main drag.

He managed ten paces before Erebus jerked up his arm and shot him in the back. As Jacques crashed face first into the dirt, Oliver slipped back into the stable and joined Gabriel and Yohann.

'Dead?' Gabriel asked.

'Sure,' Oliver said with a sigh. 'Erebus Finch came out of the saloon and shot him up.'

They both faced Yohann, who offered them a broad smile.

'Welcome,' he said, 'to Hell Town.'

5

'What did Jacques do to deserve that?' Oliver asked.

'He didn't pay his bar bill,' Yohann said.

Oliver laughed, but Yohann looked at him levelly, making him frown.

'You're not joking, are you?'

'He owed too many people too much money, so Santiago's new man dealt with him.'

'Erebus is supposed to be taming Hell Town, not punishing men for unpaid bar bills.'

Yohann narrowed his eyes. 'You know plenty for a man who's just ridden into town.'

Oliver winced, making Gabriel slap a hand on his shoulder and laugh.

'My friend,' he said jovially, 'loves gossip and all we've heard about in every saloon is Helliton's first town-tamer.'

'Erebus is the fourth.'

'My mistake.' Gabriel smiled benignly until Yohann wandered away, after which he directed Oliver to the door. He didn't speak again until they were outside and heading to the saloon. 'But *your* mistake could have cost us plenty. Think before you speak.'

'I will, but as you said, you have to expect a bartender to gossip.'

While they walked along, Santiago appeared and urged the crowd to disperse, which they did while chatting animatedly, suggesting that Yohann had been right and Jacques's demise was overdue. So Oliver put his mind to how he would secure work, and the first thing he noticed was the saloon's name.

He stomped to a halt in surprise. The saloon was called the Queen of Spades.

'What's wrong?' Gabriel asked, stopping by the door.

'I'm just nervous,' Oliver said. He mustered a smile before hurrying on to join Gabriel.

Inside, the saloon was quiet, the only

61

customers being eight men who had drawn tables together into an arrangement from which they could watch the confrontation outside. Although, when Oliver and Gabriel reached the bar, Oliver saw that this room was perfectly positioned for observation of the town and the ravine entrance.

While Gabriel attracted a quiet female bartender's attention, out in the street Santiago directed Yohann to take Jacques's body behind a building that stood beside the burnt-out wreckage.

'Another one for the pit,' someone said; a customer's comment identified him as being Murtagh Grieve. He laughed and stood up to face them. 'Which makes me wonder what you men want.'

Oliver took a deep breath. 'I'm looking for work.'

His response made the other customers swing round to face them with smirks on their faces. It also made Gabriel catch his eye with a sorry look that said he should have let him do the talking.

'That's interesting.' Murtagh beckoned and the other men scraped back their chairs and stood up. 'What kind of work are you looking for?'

'I tend bar.'

Peals of laughter rang out as some men patted each other on the back and others slapped raised legs as they enjoyed this single answer to the utmost. Oliver joined in with a snorted laugh, which made Murtagh's jovial expression tighten.

'What are you laughing at?' he demanded, walking up to Oliver.

Oliver sighed as this encounter headed in an inevitably bad direction, and he thought carefully before making his next comment.

'I'm a friendly and dutiful man who has tended bar for many years. I reckon I can be of service.'

Murtagh rubbed his bristled jaw as he considered this reply, searching for something he could take exception to.

'And so instead of staying in Prudence, you came here. Then you rode in quietly because you knew Erebus Finch was here.'

Oliver gestured at the window. 'You can see the whole town, but how do you know the rest?'

'We know everything about everyone who comes within a hundred miles of Helliton.'

Oliver couldn't think of an answer to this, but he didn't need to as Gabriel took a pace closer.

'You're an observant man,' he said, 'but we came from the east and it's a reasonable guess that we left Prudence. I gave our details at the entrance and Yohann Johanson looked like a man who passes on information quickly.'

Murtagh turned to Gabriel, his eyes narrowing with a mixture of menace and glee that someone was prepared to talk back to him.

'You saying I'm a liar?'

'I'm saying in a town like this, information is power.' Gabriel took another pace closer. 'And you're fortunate enough to be speaking to the most powerful man you'll ever meet.'

Murtagh sneered. 'You want to know what happened to the last man who made such a claim?'

'Nope.'

Murtagh folded his arms. 'He got shot to hell while you were riding into town.'

Gabriel shrugged. 'Then you should make sure the same doesn't happen to me.'

Murtagh tipped back his hat in a show of surprise at Gabriel's retorts. His surly grin told Oliver what his response would be and Gabriel had worked it out too: as when Murtagh hurled a punch at his face Gabriel thrust up an arm and deflected the blow.

With Murtagh off-balance, Gabriel grabbed his arm and helped him on his way. Even before Murtagh had hit the floor, he turned to the nearest man.

Gabriel adopted a calm expression

that gave his opponent the option of backing down, but Oliver didn't see how this encounter panned out as two men moved in on him. He raised his hands while backing away, but that didn't stop them charging him.

Oliver bunched his fists, but the men battered them aside without breaking their stride and before he could throw even a single punch one man gathered up his arms. Then he twisted him so that he could hold his hands behind his back, after which the other man grabbed the back of his head and shoved him on.

He was marched to a table where he was bent double so that his cheek was smashed down against the wood. Then he was held securely.

His captors did nothing more, but the sounds of scuffling and thuds suggested that Gabriel was fighting back with greater success than he had. One man and then another went careering backwards past Oliver's table before they fell over, having been dispatched with strong punches.

Unfortunately, several men then joined forces and, despite Gabriel's initial success, they soon ended his resistance. Scraping footfalls sounded before the table beside him rattled as Gabriel was secured in the same way as he was being held.

'Shall we take them outside?' one man asked.

'No,' Murtagh said. 'Santiago will want Erebus to deal with them.'

An affirmative grunt sounded and the men looked through the window, suggesting that Santiago and Erebus would arrive soon. Sure enough, a few moments later the doors creaked and Erebus spoke up.

'Trouble?' he asked.

'While you were dealing with Jacques,' Murtagh said, 'these men rode into town. They asked about you.'

Footfalls sounded as Erebus and Santiago walked around the tables.

'That's Gabriel Bigelow,' Santiago

said. He moved on to Oliver's table, but he gave him only a cursory glance that didn't register recognition. 'I don't know the fat one.'

Oliver slumped, feeling strangely annoyed even though he was used to the anonymity that came with being a bartender. The men holding him relaxed, accepting that he didn't present a threat, while several men moved to surround Gabriel's table.

'What shall we do with them?' Murtagh asked.

'Gabriel's a bounty hunter. Find out who he was looking for before Erebus kills him. I don't care about the fat one.'

Rough hands grabbed Oliver's shoulders and moved him to stand alongside Gabriel, who had twice the number of men holding him. Gabriel was calm and he showed no sign of planning to fight back, presumably because he was saving his strength for a more suitable moment.

They weren't taken away immediately, so Oliver caught Gabriel's eye, hoping that he'd indicate what he was thinking, but Gabriel only winked and looked past him at the stairs at the side of the saloon room. Oliver followed his gaze to note that a woman was coming down the stairs.

Their captors were watching her, and by the time she reached the bar everyone was facing her. Oliver presumed they weren't just intrigued by her low-cut bodice and short petticoats as she walked with a confident straight back that exuded authority.

'You promised me, Santiago,' she said, 'that resolving the situation with Jacques Herzog would reduce problems, not increase them.'

'It will, Priscilla,' Santiago said, his simpering tone at odds with his previous harsh attitude. 'But these newcomers were looking for trouble.'

'You know my rule: everybody leaves Helliton's troubles at the door.'

Santiago chuckled. 'I understand. I'll take them outside.'

Santiago nodded to the men holding

Gabriel, who shoved him forward, but that made Priscilla step forward.

'That's not what I meant. I gave your latest hired gun permission to remove Jacques from my establishment because his behaviour had become intolerable. I haven't given you permission to take these men away.'

Santiago and Priscilla considered each other and although Oliver was unaware of the situation in town, their resolute expressions told him that, aside from his and Gabriel's fates, an important matter was being decided.

'Of course,' Santiago said with a short bow. He stepped aside so that she could see the prisoners.

Priscilla considered Oliver without interest before she moved on to face Gabriel. A brief smile appeared.

Her reaction revealed that she knew him and that she might even have expected him, so Oliver held his breath in anticipation of her response.

'These men are my valued guests,' she declared. 'They can stay in the

Queen of Spades for as long as they wish.'

Erebus stepped forward, his eyes narrowing as his usual calm attitude died, but Santiago raised a hand, halting him. Then Santiago beckoned their captors to release them, which they did quickly before pushing them aside with firm slaps to the shoulders.

'As you wish,' Santiago said, speaking softly with exaggerated courtesy. 'While they remain your valued customers, they'll get no trouble from me.'

'I'm obliged,' she said with equally soft courtesy.

Santiago faced Gabriel and when he spoke again his tone was a low and menacing growl.

'Priscilla saved you, but my promise applies only to this saloon and you can't stay in here for ever.'

Santiago waited until Gabriel acknowledged the threat with a nod before he gestured at Erebus to join him in leaving.

Once they'd headed outside, with

face-saving posturing and good-natured chatter, Murtagh and his men returned to their tables. Without comment they resumed keeping lookout, adopting their former positions as if the confrontation had never happened.

'So your message didn't lie,' Priscilla said. She walked up to Gabriel to look him over. 'Gabriel Bigelow has come running back to me.'

'I run for no woman,' Gabriel said. 'I only wanted a way in here.'

Her eyes blazed and she swung up a hand to slap his cheek, but Gabriel caught the hand at shoulder height and held it.

'As your life depends on it,' she said, 'if you remember nothing else, remember this: I'm the most important person in town.'

'The queen of spades always was.'

She strained to lower her hand, but she couldn't move it.

'Then don't play games with me. Your message said you had something important to tell me. What is it?'

Gabriel smiled and gestured at Oliver. 'I've brought you the finest bartender in the state. He wants a job.'

The answer made her stifle a yawn with her free hand before she glanced at Oliver.

'Consider him employed. Is that all you have to offer?'

'Of course not.' Gabriel looked around the saloon before settling his gaze on the stairs. 'But not here.'

'Of course,' she said with a wink.

6

'Who is she?' Oliver asked Wilhelmina McCraw, his fellow bartender, when there was a lull in customers wanting service.

'Priscilla Helliton,' Wilhelmina said in a bored monotone.

Oliver raised an eyebrow in surprise. 'She was part of the original Helliton gang?'

'The queen of spades was the leader's woman.' Wilhelmina signified that a customer wanted serving. 'But such matters are irrelevant to a bartender.'

Oliver winked. 'On the contrary, gossip is everything to a bartender.'

She mustered a thin smile, the first he'd seen her give.

'I guess I'll have to remember that.'

Oliver dealt with the waiting customer, and when that initiated an influx of drinkers wanting liquor, he couldn't continue their conversation. Later, during another quiet period, her last comment came back to him, and he probed for more information.

'Have you not been working here for long?'

'Longer than you have,' she snapped, her narrowed eyes not inviting him to ask more questions.

'I only ask because you don't seem happy here.'

She considered him with her hands on her hips.

'This is Helliton. Why should I be happy?'

Oliver couldn't find a reply, so when she waved him away he leaned on the bar. Having adopted his usual placid expression, which registered a mixture of boredom and a willingness to serve, he studied the customers and applied his years of experience of watching frequenters of saloons.

Most of the men drank quietly in small groups as they avoided drawing attention to themselves. Oliver surmised that now the euphoria over Jacques's demise had receded, everyone was wondering who would be the next to suffer.

Erebus and Santiago sat together, Erebus watching the customers with his back to the wall. As he had done in the Hunter's Moon, he idly tossed a gold eagle and caught it on the back of his other hand, but he never once looked at the coin.

Santiago spoke animatedly to anyone who strayed close. Oliver didn't need to have seen how he'd behaved before Erebus arrived to deduce that Erebus's presence had filled him with confidence.

Murtagh's group kept lookout with a diligence that suggested they expected trouble. But as it turned out, despite the town's reputation as a lawless outlaw stronghold, the evening was no tenser than other nights in other saloons in which Oliver had served.

Although Gabriel stayed upstairs, when they needed liquor the men who had attacked him showed no further antipathy. On the contrary, Santiago and Erebus barely acknowledged his presence, so clearly he'd been identified as not representing a threat.

By midnight, when all the customers aside from Erebus and Murtagh's group had gone, Santiago walked over to Murtagh.

'Rex Amney won't return tonight,' he said.

'Agreed,' Murtagh murmured. He gestured at the other watchers to leave, which they did with sighs of relief after their long vigil.

Santiago went outside, leaving Erebus to dally and seemingly make a point that he left when he chose to, not when Santiago left.

With the saloon emptied, Oliver and Wilhelmina cleared up. Oliver heeded Wilhelmina's earlier request to be silent, although this didn't make her relax. When all was done she headed upstairs, leaving Oliver alone in the saloon room.

For the first time that evening he came out from behind the bar. Standing in the middle of the room he considered his new domain.

'It's not as good as my old saloon,' he said to himself in an attempt to cheer his spirits, 'but maybe with Trip's help it can be, one day.'

★　★　★

'We'll start at the beginning, again,' Santiago Pinchete said, his voice echoing in the dark, 'and this time I want the truth.'

'I told you the truth the first time,' Vaughan Price bleated. 'I can't tell you anything different.'

'I didn't ask you to tell me anything different.' Santiago stood at Vaughan's shoulder and leaned over to whisper in his ear through the sack. 'I just asked for the truth.'

Vaughan nodded, accepting that

Santiago was a shrewder man than he'd given him credit for during his first interrogation. Santiago had clearly remembered his story and now he planned to compare it to his latest tale, looking for differences.

This didn't cheer Vaughan; even though he'd told the truth, there were sure to be discrepancies as he was still as nervous as he had been when he'd been captured.

For the last few days he had been held captive in this room in Helliton. He had been tied to a chair with a sack over his head, so he didn't know who was holding him. Although as Tobias Swift had been killed he presumed he was being kept alive until someone in authority returned to question him.

That man had arrived today. Vaughan had told Santiago everything and he did so again.

Throughout his statement Santiago remained silent, pacing from side to side, only his crunching footfalls letting Vaughan identify his position.

'Then Tobias got shot up,' Vaughan said, finishing his tale, 'before he could follow me down into the canyon.'

'And if the secret way in to Helliton had really been secret, what would you have done next?'

Vaughan took a deep breath. 'As I told you, we would have taken the gold and escaped with it.'

Santiago stopped pacing and Vaughan sensed him leaning forward to loom over him.

'That would be the dead men's gold, would it?'

'It would.'

Santiago snarled, making Vaughan tense a moment before a scything blow slammed into the side of his head. He and the chair toppled sideways. He landed on his side with his left cheek mashed against the gritty floor and his right ear ringing. Santiago hunkered down in front of him and gripped the sack.

He gathered handfuls of the cloth to draw the sack tightly around Vaughan's throat until the weave was pressed so close to his face that he could make out Santiago's outline.

'Try again,' Santiago whispered.

'I can't give you no other answer, because that's the truth. We came here to find the dead men's gold and if we hadn't been discovered, we would have got away with it.'

'That would be the gold stolen by the Helliton gang ten years ago and which, after they were all killed, has never been seen again? A stash that has become legend and which, because everyone connected to it died, has become known as the dead men's gold?'

Vaughan nodded eagerly, although that made the sack constrict around his throat, stopping his movement.

'The legend also says the bones of a hundred men lie scattered around the gold because everyone who has ever gone looking for it has died too.'

'The fate of your companion would suggest the final part of the legend has some truth.'

Santiago loosened his grip. Then, with a grunt as if he'd made a decision, he righted the chair and set Vaughan back upright. Then he resumed pacing, letting Vaughan presume he was about to be given the obvious ultimatum that Tobias had first given him.

When several minutes passed without Santiago delivering it, Vaughan couldn't stop himself speaking.

'Why are you so dismissive of the legend?'

Santiago grunted with seeming approval of this question.

'Because in the two years I've been here so many men have come looking for it that I can believe a hundred men have died on the hopeless quest, but I intend to consign such madness to Helliton's past. Our future will be free from outlaws and ranting madmen who come in search of cursed gold.'

'I'm no madman.'

'I can see that.'

Vaughan sighed, now realizing that Santiago was deliberately avoiding asking the obvious question, presumably as a test. As he doubted whether anything else he could say would save him, he looked at Santiago as he paced, and put on as confident a tone as he could manage.

'I can resolve your problem for you. Let me go and I'll leave with the gold. Then nobody will ever come looking for it again.'

Santiago chuckled. 'So you're confident you know where it is?'

'Yes.'

'Then you're more stupid than I thought.' Santiago stopped pacing. 'Did you really think nobody had thought to look down the well?'

For the first time Vaughan was pleased the sack was over his head, as he couldn't stop himself wincing.

'The information I was given said that nobody had looked.'

Santiago snorted with irritation, then with rapid steps he paced up to him. This time he punched Vaughan in the mouth, sending him rocking back in his chair.

The chair didn't topple, so Santiago slapped his cheek. When the chair still didn't fall over, he planted a foot against Vaughan's chest and pushed him over.

Vaughan landed on his back where he lay flexing his jaw and tasting blood.

'The well is in the centre of town,' Santiago said, standing over him. 'Everybody goes there and as it's our only water supply, whenever trouble erupts it's the most strategically important place in town. Yet somehow you believe that in all those years, nobody has thought to look into it and see the gold that was dropped down there?'

Vaughan gulped. 'So the well is in the centre of town. I didn't know that.'

'Everyone knows they built the town around it. You planned to sneak in unseen with your rope, lower yourself down the well, and escape with the gold?'

'That was the plan.'

'And that's why I don't believe you.' Santiago tapped a boot against his side.

'A heap of trouble is heading Helliton's way and thankfully I have a hired gun who can deal with it. Once Erebus Finch has installed peace, he'll relish getting the truth out of you. So when I return, make sure you have a better explanation of what you want and who you work for or I'll hand you over to him.'

Vaughan didn't reply. After pacing around him twice Santiago righted his chair. Then he left the room, leaving Vaughan to think how he could use the information he'd been given to bargain for his life.

'They built the town around the well,' he said to himself, 'apparently.'

Despite his bruised cheek and lips, beneath the sack he smiled as for the first time he understood the full truth behind the legend of the dead men's gold.

7

When a crick in the neck woke Oliver up it was light.

Last night nobody had told him whether a room was available, so he had slept on a shelf beneath the bar. After a long and tiring day, the moment he had rested his head he had fallen into a deep sleep.

Come the morning light he was still alone, so he wandered around the saloon, getting a feel for the place that had become his new home.

He stopped at the window from where, Murtagh's men being absent, he considered the view properly for the first time. First light was spreading across the eastern sky providing enough light to let him see that nobody else had stirred yet.

Last night Santiago had threatened only Gabriel, but although leaving the saloon could still be dangerous, at this early hour he risked slipping outside. He wandered away from the saloon and even though the main drag was, seemingly, deserted he felt uneasy, as if he were being watched.

He was about to scurry back inside when his gaze alighted on the burnt-out building. He hadn't heard anybody talking about this place's fate. Feeling curious, he sidled towards the wreckage.

The closer he got the more it resembled his own burnt-out saloon. When he reached the heap of blackened wood he even found a largely intact bar along with tables and chairs.

As the Queen of Spades was the only saloon in town, Oliver presumed this saloon's destruction explained why it had been so crowded last night. As he found nothing of interest, he turned back.

He winced. While he'd been distracted Yohann Johanson had stirred and was now standing by the only door into the saloon, watching him.

As he had to seek entry past him, Oliver moved on. After he'd taken a few paces the ostler called out to him.

'It's your good fortune you didn't arrive a week earlier,' he said. 'You could have been working there.'

Oliver didn't reply until he reached the door, devising a response that wouldn't give him problems later, bearing in mind Gabriel's theory that Yohann passed on information quickly.

'I'm content working where I am,' he said.

'As am I.' Yohann nodded, considering him. 'You don't look like the men who usually ride into Hell Town.'

Oliver noted Yohann's wizened frame and lopsided smile.

'Neither do you.'

'It's safest not to. I've been here for five years and nobody notices me. Men come and go and battles over territory and money and women are fought, but me, I just keep the stables clean and my horses fed and watered. No matter what happens today, that's what I'll be doing tomorrow.'

'You reckon today might bring trouble?'

'Rex Amney will return soon and Santiago has a new hired gun, but that's not my point. I don't think about trouble and trouble don't think about me.'

'That's good advice.' Oliver joined Yohann and for some moments the two men stood looking down the main drag, their silence acknowledging their shared attitude. Then Oliver asked, 'What kind of trouble happened to the other saloon?'

'The same thing that happened to the rest. We once had four saloons, but we lost one and then another. Now we have one large building.' Yohann snorted a rueful laugh. 'Which sums up the history of Hell Town.'

'I understand what you mean,' Oliver said in a conversational manner.

Yohann saw that Oliver was looking at the first intact building on the main drag. He pointed at it.

'That's Santiago's office. He owns that side of town. Now that Jacques Herzog's been dealt with, Rex owns the other side, for now.'

They stood in silence. Oliver figured that if he probed too deeply Yohann would clam up, as Wilhelmina had done last night, and his comments would reach Santiago. On the other hand, unless he took chances, he'd never learn anything.

'If you've been here for five years,' he said, leaning towards Yohann and adopting a casual tone, 'you must have met Trip Kincaid.'

Yohann winced and he stared at him in horror.

'What did you go and say that for?'

'Trip's my brother.'

'Then that's even worse. I knew I shouldn't have spoken to you.'

Yohann waved a dismissive hand at him and turned on his heel. As he shuffled away, he shook his head sadly while muttering to himself.

Oliver was tempted to run after him and demand an explanation, but he doubted Yohann would speak openly again and the growing light was encouraging more people to stir.

He headed back into the saloon where he embarked on the morning ritual he'd adopted in his own saloon of rubbing down tables and mopping the floor. The task relaxed him and stopped him dwelling on what Yohann's reaction had meant, so by mid-morning he was whistling to himself when Wilhelmina led several saloon girls downstairs.

The women sat at a table while Wilhelmina went behind the bar. Then they all considered him with bleary-eyed bemusement, as if nobody had ever cleaned the saloon before.

The stained floor and furniture suggested nobody ever had, but Oliver kept that thought to himself. Although there were no offers of help he worked until Priscilla and Gabriel arrived.

'I told you he was the finest bartender in the state,' Gabriel said with a proud smile.

'He's certainly the cleanest,' Priscilla said with approval. She led the saloon girls into a back room, presumably to give them instructions for the new day.

Gabriel sat at the end of the bar until Murtagh Grieve and his men arrived. Gabriel tensed, but other than avoiding meeting his eye, Murtagh ignored him while Oliver served coffee.

For the next three hours Oliver leaned on the bar in a position from where he could watch the scene outside. Few people ventured outside, and those who did looked at the ravine entrance before they hurried to the well, collected water quickly, and then sped out of view.

The one man not to scurry into hiding was Erebus Finch, who left his office on Santiago's side of town and took a leisurely stroll towards the saloon.

On the way Santiago joined him and they chatted animatedly while smiling, seemingly making a show of being relaxed. When they arrived at the saloon they came to the bar and Santiago demanded coffees.

Oliver had become used to them ignoring him, so when he returned with full mugs he winced on noticing that Erebus was considering him oddly.

'I have met you before,' Erebus mused. 'When?'

'Last night,' Oliver said. 'I didn't think you'd had that much to drink.'

'You're a funny man.' Erebus's sombre tone suggested otherwise.

The exchange made Santiago consider Oliver with his eyes narrowed, then he shook his head.

'All bartenders look the same to me,' he declared, cradling his mug and leaning back against the bar.

'This one's different,' Erebus said.

Santiago shrugged, but Erebus continued looking at him, making Oliver nervously clean the bar. Then Oliver smiled.

'I tend bar and I'm free with information,' Oliver said. He pointed at the window. 'And right now I can tell you some men are riding into town.'

A moment later Murtagh noticed the approaching riders too. Pointing, he leapt to his feet, making Santiago slap his mug down on the bar and spilled coffee before hurrying to join Murtagh at the window.

Erebus stayed to stare at Oliver, letting him know he'd noted his relief at the fortuitously timed distraction. When he sauntered off to consider the situation, Gabriel left to fetch Priscilla.

'If that's Rex,' she called when she came through the door, 'you won't confront him in here.'

'If he comes in here, he may force my hand,' Santiago said, turning round. 'Remember, he has nowhere else to go after his favourite saloon burnt down.'

His men laughed, leaving Oliver in no doubt as to who had been responsible; it also made Wilhelmina mutter under her breath before she scurried to the back room. Priscilla tried to bar her way, and when she failed she hurried after her, leaving Gabriel standing opposite Oliver at the bar, from where they watched four riders move towards town.

Oliver got confirmation that Rex had arrived when Santiago caught Erebus's eye and nodded. At the signal Erebus headed outside, after which Santiago gestured at Murtagh, who led his men after him.

Finally, Santiago left, leaving only Gabriel and Oliver in the saloon room.

'It looks,' Gabriel said, 'as if the Queen of Spades will be the safest place in town.'

Oliver smiled. 'Why do you think I became a bartender?'

'At times like this I enjoy being a customer.' Gabriel said nothing more until Rex approached the edge of town; then glancing to either side to confirm that nobody could hear him, he asked, 'Learnt anything about Trip yet?'

'Nothing other than that he came here.'

'I've heard nothing too, but if I learn

anything, I'll let you know.' Gabriel frowned. 'Anyone talk about Priscilla?'

'Only to reveal her full name. How do you know her?'

'I went after the Helliton gang ten years ago. I never got close to them. I did get close to her.'

Oliver laughed. 'I gathered that much.'

'I wouldn't have sought her out again if I didn't think I could find the gold.' Gabriel lowered his voice to a whisper. 'But even if the message I sent her got me in, I'm sure she won't help me leave.'

'I can't help you with that, but if I find a way, I'll let you know.' He waited until Gabriel smiled, then gestured at the window. 'Who would you prefer to survive this showdown?'

'Priscilla and Santiago have forged an understanding, but I don't reckon that'll last if Rex is killed. On the other hand, if Rex prevails, he's not as ambitious as Santiago is, so he might not confront her. And you?'

Oliver rubbed his chin. 'I don't care who survives. In fact, as a quieter town will help me investigate, the best result would be if Erebus and Rex wiped each other out.'

'Agreed.'

Wilhelmina came out of the back room then and they reverted to silence. Gabriel watched the scene outside while Oliver cleaned glasses.

Wilhelmina loitered behind the bar, seemingly preoccupied. Her eyes were puffy, presumably from crying, and she was as quiet as always.

With a sigh she went over to the window, where she peered outside with a fist clenched and tapping against her hip. Then she nodded, as if she'd made a decision, and walked to the door.

'It's not safe out there,' Oliver called after her.

She didn't acknowledge him and slipped outside. When she came into view through the window she was edging away from the saloon one cautious pace at a time.

Further down the main drag Erebus was leaning on his office wall. His right hand rocked up and down as he tossed a coin.

Santiago's men moved towards the well while Rex stopped fifty yards from the edge of town. Two riders joined him from behind, suggesting the ravine guards had sided with him.

Santiago stood at the corner, where he would be close enough to watch the showdown but far enough away to avoid trouble.

'I guess,' Gabriel said when he noted that Oliver was watching Wilhelmina, 'it must be hard on her being only a bartender now.'

'I didn't know she was once anything more.'

'She owned the burnt-out saloon.' Gabriel gestured towards the canyon side. 'And she welcomed Rex's company.'

Gabriel raised an eyebrow and Oliver nodded as another aspect of the situation became apparent.

'Women have done well in Hell Town.'

'The womenfolk of the outlaws who holed up here all survived for longer than their men did and they gained some control over the town. Apparently there were once four of them. Everyone called them the queens, but Wilhelmina and Priscilla are the last of them.'

Oliver gripped tightly the glass he was cleaning as his heart raced.

'Does that mean the saloon that got burnt down was called the Queen of Hearts?'

'It was.'

'Which means Wilhelmina is also known as the Queen of Hearts?'

Gabriel shrugged. 'I guess she is.'

8

Gabriel considered Oliver oddly but, as Wilhelmina was already fifty yards away, he didn't explain what had concerned him. Oliver came out from behind the bar and strode to the window.

Outside, more men emerged from Rex's side of town and this encouraged Rex to move on. While Santiago's men gathered around Murtagh, Wilhelmina hurried on until she mingled in with the men facing them.

Erebus stayed apart from the groups, but despite the numerous people who were outside, it was clear who was siding with whom. Rex's men were on the left side of town and Santiago's men were on the right.

As both groups eyed each other, a showdown was clearly imminent, so Oliver took a deep breath. Then, with a glance at the bemused Gabriel, he made for the door.

'Stay here,' Gabriel shouted after him. 'The middle of a showdown isn't the right time to ask Wilhelmina about the name of her saloon.'

'This may be my only chance.'

Gabriel considered him with consternation, then he shrugged showing he wouldn't try to stop him; Oliver slipped outside and stood against the wall.

Two men were talking with Wilhelmina and their gestures towards the saloon suggested they were telling her to leave, but she ignored them and moved on until Rex saw her.

Rex nodded to her and they exchanged a few words before he dismounted at the first building. This brief conversation appeared to satisfy her, for she made her way back.

Since Rex and his men were lining up to consider the forces aligned against them Oliver reckoned she'd had the right idea and he turned back to the saloon. He'd taken a single pace when gunfire erupted.

He flinched and went to one knee with his head lowered, using a movement he'd employed whenever gunfire erupted in his saloon. When the gunshots continued to rattle away, all at the opposite end of town, he looked over his shoulder.

Some men were fleeing for cover with their heads down; others backed away while still shooting. In the frantic confusion Oliver couldn't work out which group was likely to prevail and, worse, he couldn't see Wilhelmina.

He got to his feet and edged forward until he perceived her cowering behind the low wall that surrounded the circular well. As she might be the best person to solve the mystery of Trip's disappearance, he watched her anxiously while shuffling forward.

Two of Santiago's men dived into cover behind the well. A few moments later they raised themselves to trade gunfire with Rex's men, who went to ground amidst the buildings on their side of town.

When the rest of Santiago's men scurried into hiding on their side, they left only two men lying shot and still between the two groups, suggesting it would take a while to resolve the showdown.

'A man like you,' Santiago called from outside his office, 'should stay in the saloon until this is over.'

The fact that Santiago was keeping out of the trouble he had instigated combined with confirmation that his threat last night had applied only to Gabriel made Oliver mutter to himself in irritation.

Anger at his inability to help Wilhelmina and the fact that nobody considered him to be worth threatening overcame his fear and he strode towards the well. His anger kept him moving for fifty determined paces until a stray bullet sliced into the dirt two yards to his left, sending up a flurry of dust and bringing him to his senses.

He shook himself and, feeling vulnerable, scampered away to take cover in the gap between two buildings. He stayed out of sight as a volley of gunshots tore out and then retaliatory gunfire blasted.

When an uncomfortable silence had continued for a minute, he edged forward and glanced around, taking in the length of the main drag.

Gabriel was standing in the saloon doorway watching him in bemusement, while Santiago had moved out of view. No gunmen were visible, so the only other person he could see was Wilhelmina; she was on her haunches and swaying anxiously as she readied herself to run to safety.

Hunched over she shuffled away towards the edge of town. She moved slowly, presumably to make it clear she wasn't a threat.

Even so, after three paces one of Santiago's gunmen emerged briefly from a building opposite and fired at her. The slug kicked dust at her feet, and that encouraged Rex's men to shoot at the gunman.

As shots hammered into the wooden wall behind which the gunman was hiding, Wilhelmina dug in a heel and dived back behind the well. She lay on her chest with her head buried in her folded arms, looking as if she wouldn't risk fleeing again.

Oliver reckoned if she stayed there she'd be safe but, the gunfire all being directed at one building, Murtagh and another gunman used the distraction to run for the well. They covered half the distance before Rex's men reacted.

Wild gunfire hit the dirt to either side of the running men, but before the shooters could get them in their sights the men dived to the ground and scrambled into hiding beside the men who were already there. The rapid gunfire continued with shots clattering into the stone wall and to either side, keeping them and Wilhelmina pinned down.

As soon as the fusillade died down

the men ventured around the circular wall and, lying on their chests, they started shooting. Within moments their gunfire subdued Rex's men and three more of Santiago's men hurried to the well.

When these men had holed up, the group fired at Rex's position. Despite the rattling gunfire, Oliver heard two cries of pain. Heartened, Santiago's men edged away from the well as they prepared to run towards Rex.

As it looked as though Rex would be overrun Erebus appeared for the first time since the showdown had started. He ran towards three barrels opposite Oliver where he knelt down to appraise the situation.

Erebus glanced at Oliver before he examined the scene two buildings down from him. What he saw there made him rest his gun on the top of a barrel and take careful aim.

He didn't fire, so Oliver assumed he was waiting until he could get a clear shot at Rex. A few moments later he was proved right when Rex led a group of four men out of the building.

The men ran towards Santiago's men while Rex made for the well, possibly to rescue Wilhelmina, but he had covered only five paces before Erebus fired. His shot ripped into Rex's chest and made him drop to his knees.

Wilhelmina screeched in distress as Rex swayed, but then Erebus downed him with a shot to the side. Rex's men kept running and another group from further down the main drag joined them as in a coordinated action they assailed Santiago's men, using a pincer movement.

Wilhelmina was trapped in the middle of this gun-fight. She lay rigidly on her front, making it uncertain whether she had been wounded or was too petrified and distressed to move.

Whatever the reason, Oliver doubted she would survive the gun battle unscathed. Without thinking he edged out from between the buildings. Then he started walking towards the well.

His heart raced and he struggled to breathe, so that with every breath he heard an odd clicking sound in his throat. He raised his hands to show he was unarmed, but as that was unlikely to be heeded, he speeded up as he committed himself to his unwise rescue attempt.

Ahead, the two groups blasted lead at each other, thankfully ignoring him. Since the two groups were only twenty yards apart he would have to cut across their gunfire to reach Wilhelmina, and then again when leaving, so he doubted he'd be ignored for much longer.

When he reached Rex's body the magnitude of the task hit him. He dropped to one knee and without thinking he grabbed Rex's six-shooter, which was lying beside the body's outstretched hand.

He'd never fired a weapon in his life so, as gunfire blasted out ahead, he hefted the six-shooter on his clammy palm and examined it. Then with a loud gulp and his heart hammering, he got to his feet and moved on.

Oliver was thirty paces from the well when a gunman noticed him. The man was on Rex's side, so Oliver aimed the gun at Santiago's men, making the man look away and ensuring Oliver didn't have to shoot.

He'd gone five paces further when one of Santiago's men faced him, so he aimed at Rex's men, which appeared to satisfy the man. As Oliver doubted such subterfuge would work for much longer, he decided his best option was to make his intentions clear.

'Wilhelmina!' he shouted. 'I'm getting you out of there.'

His cry was loud enough to make Wilhelmina raise her head, although she looked at him with bewilderment. He sensed gunmen on either side considering him with equal bemusement, but he'd set himself on this course of action and he couldn't veer away from it now.

He lowered his head and as fast as his short legs would carry him he ran for the well. With every pace he expected someone to cut him down, but even though the sporadic shooting continued, he closed on the well unharmed.

From the corner of his eye he saw movement. To his left Rex's men were hunkering down in positions where they could pin down Santiago's men and to his right Santiago's men were scrambling into hiding.

As he could no longer hear shooting over his hoarse breathing, clearly there was a lull in the gun-fight. He doubted it would last for long, so he thrust his head down even lower and sprinted so hard that his ankles cracked with every pace, making it sound as if his legs were in danger of breaking.

At this speed he struggled to keep his balance and, with his arms pumping, his progress became more frantic until the inevitable happened and he slipped and toppled forward.

He went to his knees, skidded, bounced back up to gain his feet before he again tumbled over and hit the ground. This time he didn't get up: he skidded along on his chest until his momentum made him roll.

The well, the main drag and the gunmen appeared to spin around him until with a jarring thud he fetched up against the wall. A hand grabbed his shoulder and sought to move him. He tried to bat it away, but the hand only gripped him more tightly.

When his vision stopped swirling, he saw that Wilhelmina had touched him. She was looking at him with concern and, purely by luck, he'd come to rest with his back set against the stone wall beside her.

'What are you doing?' she said, aghast.

'I'm rescuing you,' Oliver gasped with a hand to his chest as he willed his racing heart to slow. 'That's what I'm doing.'

'Why?' She waited for an answer, which Oliver couldn't provide, then she gestured at him. 'You look like you need rescuing more than I do.'

Oliver shrugged. 'Either way, we bartenders should look out for each other.'

He gave a tentative smile that she didn't return.

'You're either the bravest man I've ever met or the most stupid.'

'It's probably the second one.'

She smiled before looking around for an escape route, his arrival galvanizing her into action, but before she could act the lull in firing ended and the gunmen on either side of the well started shooting. Oliver shook himself to regain his senses and moved to get to his feet.

Unfortunately the madness that had overcome him and let him run to the well had evaporated. He couldn't make his legs work and he managed only to tip over and knock into Wilhelmina. So he used his blunder to slap her back and push her to the ground.

She didn't object and as gunfire blasted they both lay cringing and making themselves as small as possible. They lay still until someone cried out in pain only feet away, making Oliver risk looking up.

While a gunman crumpled to the ground to lie over another shot man, another gunman ran for cover, the attempt by Rex's men to seize control of the well having failed. Then rapid footfalls sounded as Santiago's men advanced while Murtagh ran along the wall whooping in triumph.

Murtagh was aiming at a fleeing gunman, but he saw Oliver, with Wilhelmina lying beneath him, so he swung his gun down to aim at Wilhelmina. Oliver jerked to the left while pushing Wilhelmina to the right, an action he didn't carry out strongly enough as she didn't move.

It took Oliver a moment to realize he hadn't pushed her effectively because he was still clutching Rex's gun. Luckily Wilhelmina took evasive action of her own and she rolled away.

Without thinking Oliver raised the gun. It took him a seemingly inordinate amount of time to cock and aim, but

Murtagh ignored him, following Wilhelmina's moving form with his gun.

Oliver fired, and from only a few feet away even he couldn't miss his target. Although he had aimed at Murtagh's chest, his shot sliced up into Murtagh's side, making him twitch.

As his gun fell from his hand, Murtagh swayed while looking around for the man who had shot him until his eyes lowered to light upon Oliver. He sneered in apparent disappointment before toppling over to lie sprawled over the top of the wall.

In horror Oliver stared at Murtagh's form, then he prodded his shoulder. His touch made Murtagh's arm slide off the wall and rock back and forth twice, with the fingers brushing the ground.

The fingers twitched and stilled, a sight that made Oliver accept with a gulp that he'd done the one thing he'd never expected he would do: he had shot and killed a man.

9

The sight of Murtagh's body shocked Oliver so much that it blurred his vision, while the gunfire sounded as if it were away in the distance.

He struggled to focus on his surroundings and the next he knew, he was standing up. All he could focus on was Wilhelmina, who was crawling away from the well.

He stumbled after her, his legs feeling leaden, as if he'd never walked before. Worse, before he could act he had to work out the motions required to bend down and sweep an arm beneath her stomach.

Thankfully, she worked out what he was trying to do and got to her feet. Then, she helping him as much as he was helping her, they moved towards the saloon.

Men were scurrying about around

them, but they were just blurs to him. He and Wilhelmina had managed a dozen awkward strides when a man loomed up close.

The man was looking past them, but to Oliver in his confused state his presence was as shocking as Murtagh's had been. This time Oliver didn't struggle to fire: he blasted a shot into the man's side although, as with Murtagh, he had been aiming a foot higher, and the man twisted before he toppled over.

Even when the man hit the ground he looked past Oliver, presumably thinking someone else had shot him. When the man's forehead pressed down into the dirt, Oliver looked where he had been looking.

Erebus was walking past him, proving he had been the man's intended target. He contemplated the shot man before nodding at Oliver in mocking salute.

Then Erebus moved on and Oliver, having conquered his distaste for shooting men, followed him with the intention of taking revenge.

While recalling an image of Newton's body, he aimed at Erebus's back and he would have fired, but Wilhelmina dragged him on and the moment was lost. Within moments he lost sight of Erebus amongst the scurrying gunmen, but he did see open space ahead.

Wilhelmina must have seen the route to freedom too, as she redoubled her efforts and, with the thought that he might survive hitting him for the first time, he moved more freely. They speeded up and within a few paces they were running.

They stopped holding on to each other and ran separately, which let her get ahead of him. Then, as he had done when running towards the well, Oliver stared at the saloon and ignored everything else.

After his exertions his wheezing breath burned his throat and his chest was so tight he felt ready to vomit. But with his back feeling like a target, he pounded on and with every pace the gunfire receded.

By the time he reached Santiago's office Wilhelmina was approaching the saloon door. Gabriel ushered her on before he directed Oliver inside.

Gabriel looked into his eyes, his concerned expression clearly showing he wanted to talk, but when the safety of the saloon was so close Oliver didn't care what he or anyone else wanted of him.

He ran to the door and burst inside. Then with a cry of delight he threw himself to one side, removing the last chance that someone would shoot him in the back.

He noted that Wilhelmina was standing before the window, seemingly still shocked about Rex's demise, then he staggered towards the bar. With safety assured his legs felt as if they'd no longer support him and he lurched on like a man who'd drunk most of the saloon's stock of liquor.

After ten faltering paces, he bellied up to the bar. He ran his fingertips over the wood, enjoying the feel of a sticky patch, and he smiled when he identified the stain as the one Santiago's coffee had made earlier.

He stretched out his left arm, gripped the edge of the bar and drew himself on. Then, with his body bent double so that one cheek brushed the bar, he worked his way to the end, while always keeping a hand on the wood.

When he slipped behind the bar he shuffled sideways until he'd returned to the position he'd adopted for the last day, but which already felt comfortingly familiar and which he vowed never to leave again.

Only then did he straighten up. With a deep breath he tried to engender a feeling that he was just a bartender, that this was any other day, and to dismiss the fact that he'd just killed two men.

This thought reminded him he was still clutching Rex's gun. With a disgusted yelp he snapped open his hand, letting the gun tumble away and land with a clatter on the bar. Then he rooted around for a towel and glasses.

He lined up the glasses and, using a vigorous action, he started cleaning them.

'Those glasses are already clean,' Gabriel said, moving away from the door.

'I'm making them cleaner,' Oliver said, holding a glass up to the light.

From the bar Gabriel watched the scene outside. Sporadic gunfire was still rattling away, but Oliver concentrated on each glass to block out the noise and to avoid the temptation of looking to see how the gun battle was progressing.

'You know,' Gabriel said, 'you could well be the bravest man I've ever met.'

'Wilhelmina said something like that, but I told her she was wrong. I'm the stupidest.'

'You were both right.'

Gabriel smiled, but Oliver didn't take the opportunity to lighten his mood. Instead he put down the last glass and set to work on another batch of clean glasses.

'Would you like a drink,' Oliver snapped, 'or are you just going to grin at me?'

'I've seen every reaction both before and after gunfights from detachment, to nervous activity through to panic. You're no different.'

'Which is the problem.' Oliver slammed down a glass. 'I thought I *was* different. I thought I was just a bartender, not a gunslinger.'

'After what you did, I reckon you're both.' Gabriel chuckled. 'And think of it this way, now you've charged through town blasting everyone who stood in your way to hell, nobody will ever fail to pay their bar bill again.'

This time Oliver mustered a snorted laugh, but he wasn't willing to dismiss what he'd done so readily and he resumed a stern expression while cleaning glasses. Gabriel stopped trying to cheer him up, but Wilhelmina, who had clearly listened to their conversation, now left the window.

Oliver glanced past her and observed

that it was now quiet outside. Santiago was heading away to talk to Erebus, so presumably the showdown had ended, and the result had been a bad one for Rex's side.

'If you won't tell him why you did that,' Wilhelmina said with her head tilted to one side and her expression still as incredulous as it had been when she was outside the saloon, 'you have to tell me.'

Oliver took a deep breath, devising and rejecting several answers until he settled for the simplest explanation.

'You never asked my name,' he said. 'I'm Oliver Kincaid.'

She looked perplexed until her eyes flickered with understanding.

'Ah,' she said. 'In that case I'm sorry.'

Wilhelmina came round the bar, where she helped Oliver finish cleaning glasses, her action an obvious delaying tactic that gave her time to think. Oliver didn't mind as he wasn't in the right frame of mind for conversation, but by the time they'd completed the task, her last comment had registered.

'Why are you sorry?' he asked.

She frowned. 'I'm guessing you don't know, but Trip is dead.'

Oliver lowered his head and leaned on the bar as he digested information that did at least stop him dwelling on his behaviour during the gunfight.

'I assumed he was, but I didn't know for sure.'

'He seemed a good man.' Wilhelmina adopted his posture of leaning on the bar. 'I'm sorry for what happened.'

'What did happen?' Oliver waited, but Wilhelmina glanced at Gabriel with an obvious, silent question, and so he smiled. 'I trust him and no matter what you tell me, he won't cause you any problems.'

Wilhelmina still looked around before she spoke, then she did so quietly.

'Santiago brought him here,' she said. She considered him with concern as if she expected an outburst.

'Are you saying Santiago killed my brother?'

'I didn't see him do it, but he took Trip into his office.' She frowned. 'I didn't see him again.'

'But you remember Trip's name, so you must know more.'

She frowned and again she looked around until with a nod she appeared to accept that she had to tell him everything. In a rush she blurted out her story.

'Eighteen months ago Trip came to the Queen of Hearts. He'd talked his way into town to play in a high-stakes poker game. With one hand he won a gold coin along with a story about how the owner acquired it.'

'From the dead men's gold?' Gabriel asked, interrupting their conversation. His raised eyebrow suggested he'd already guessed the answer.

'So the owner claimed, and he soon regretted it. Santiago's obsessed with finding the stash. He had the losing player killed and went looking for Trip.

When he found him he brought him back here, but he didn't get the gold.'

'How do you know that?'

'Because he's still here. Now he's trying to clean up Helliton to eliminate any rivals who might find it first. A man with information like Trip had, even when it was only a small piece of the picture, would never have stood a chance.'

'Neither will anyone else who knows something about it, I assume.'

Oliver glanced at Gabriel, but he didn't take the opportunity to explain what he knew.

'Even a hint that someone knows something is fatal.' She sighed. 'My customers had been swapping tales about the gold. I doubt anyone knew anything, but the place got burnt down. I don't know what I'd have done if Priscilla hadn't taken me in.'

Her story told Wilhelmina returned to the window, leaving the two men to stand in silence, Gabriel watching Oliver, presumably for his reaction.

The double shock of his actions outside and Wilhelmina's news had numbed him, and Oliver tried to lose himself in familiar activities. As he reckoned that the quiet scene outside meant customers would arrive soon expecting liquor, he lined up the clean glasses.

Gabriel picked up the gun that Oliver had discarded. With a finger he dragged it along to place it before Oliver.

'You know what you have to do,' Gabriel said.

'I'm never picking up a gun again,' Oliver said, reinforcing his point by gripping a glass.

'Santiago's no gunslinger.' Gabriel waited but Oliver didn't reply. 'He's hiding behind Erebus. You just have to — '

'I didn't come here for revenge,' Oliver snapped. 'I just wanted to know what happened to Trip.'

'But you now know what you can do when you have a gun. You've proved you're just as tough as I am.'

'Perhaps I don't want to be a man like you.' Oliver glanced over Gabriel's shoulder and then gestured for him to move aside. 'I tend bar and I'll soon have customers to serve.'

Gabriel turned to see that Erebus was leading the gunfight survivors along the main drag while a team of men stayed back to gather the bodies together. He turned back with his brow furrowed.

'Are you saying you wish you hadn't shot up those men?'

'I had no choice. I had to shoot them. But that doesn't mean I feel good about it.'

Gabriel slapped a hand on his shoulder and gripped it.

'In that case,' he whispered, 'you'll be pleased to know you didn't shoot anyone.'

'What are you . . . ?' Oliver trailed off as he took in Gabriel's earnest gaze. Then he looked aloft and he cast his mind back.

He had fired at Murtagh from only a

few feet away, but his aim had been poor. Strangely, he had caught Murtagh in the side and he had died quickly, even though from Oliver's position the wound would have been glancing.

The second man had suffered the same fate: a gunshot in the side even though Oliver had been facing him. Oliver gulped and looked at Gabriel with a raised eyebrow, feeling unwilling to voice the question.

Gabriel winked and drew him closer so they could talk without Wilhelmina hearing them.

'You're a bartender, not a killer.'

Oliver gulped to moisten his dry throat. 'You mean you saved my life by shooting those men from the opposite end of town?'

'It wasn't exactly like that. I left the saloon to get a better view of the gunfight. I hoped that in the confusion I might get a safe shot at Erebus.' Gabriel rubbed his jaw. 'Saving you was incidental.'

'I'm obliged, but you probably saved

Erebus's life. The second man wasn't aiming to kill me.'

'I saw that, but I'll deal with Erebus in my own time and in my own way.' Gabriel glanced through the window. Santiago had fetched Yohann to supervise taking the bodies to the pit where apparently all bodies were dumped, while Erebus would arrive in a matter of moments. 'And now you know the truth, you can deal with Santiago in your own time and in your own way.'

'I won't do that. I'm just a — '

'Don't say that again. Nobody but us two knows what really happened. As far as everyone else is concerned, you're a man to be reckoned with.'

Oliver watched as Erebus and the other victorious gunmen came inside, while outside Santiago disappeared from view.

Despite his resolution to avoid thinking about revenge, the sight of the two men who had killed people close to him made his stomach lurch. He put down the glass he was holding in case he broke it in his tight grip.

'And that,' he said, 'is supposed to make me feel better, is it?'

10

After the gunfight the survivors were in the mood to celebrate, so it was early evening before Oliver got his first break.

His gloomy prediction had turned out to be correct: he didn't feel any better about the situation. Finding out that he was capable of killing men had been bad enough, but finding out that he was so incompetent that he couldn't defend himself was worse.

With Rex Amney defeated and with everyone in good spirits, nobody had questioned his role although, as the day had worn on, men had often glanced at him, suggesting that as they pieced together the events his actions were being considered.

Erebus had sat alone, although for the first time he hadn't repeatedly tossed and caught a coin, and he hadn't spoken until Santiago arrived.

'Have a proper rest,' Wilhelmina said, eyeing Oliver with concern. 'I can deal with them for a while.'

'Don't worry about me,' Oliver said. 'Although perhaps I should worry about you. Rex appeared to be important to you.'

She shrugged. 'He was just a good customer. I tried to warn him off to stop the bloodshed.'

She didn't meet his eye, showing she wasn't being truthful, but as he didn't like to consider her being close to the man who had burned down his saloon, he didn't pry.

'In a way that has happened. There's nobody left to oppose Santiago.'

'Until he claims the gold there'll always be trouble.'

With a nod Oliver accepted Wilhelmina's original offer. While nobody was looking at him, he hurried across the room, slipped outside, and moved into the darkness beyond the window.

He stood beside the burnt-out Queen of Hearts ensuring that if anyone saw him they'd think he was examining the wreckage while from the corner of his eye he looked at Santiago's office.

Trip had been taken there, after which nobody had seen him again. He doubted he'd find evidence of what had happened to him in there, but he had to look.

Aside from a light in the stable and a glow at the ravine entrance, he saw no signs of life, so, feeling confident he wasn't being watched, he headed to the office. While watching the saloon and keeping in the shadows, he walked casually around the corner, looking like a man embarking on a stroll.

He reached a door and with a lurch, as if he'd stumbled, he put a shoulder to it. The door rattled and held, but it moved enough to give him confidence that he could break in if he needed to.

As he couldn't find any other doors he doubled back. Through the saloon window he saw the customers milling around, but nobody was watching him, so he slammed his shoulder to the door.

This time he burst in, stumbling for several paces until he crashed into a pile of posts. Quickly he closed the door and, with his heart thudding from exertion and from fear of discovery, he waited.

Several minutes passed without anyone coming to investigate and he surveyed the darkened room. It was filled with posts, ropes and wooden platforms. Clearly Santiago was storing equipment to construct something, although Oliver couldn't work out what he planned to build.

Behind a heap of pulleys a door faced him and, no longer hearing his racing heartbeat, he detected a faint noise which, after he'd strained his hearing, sounded like a child whimpering. He went to the door and listened until he concluded that the sound was that of someone breathing raggedly.

The perturbing thought hit him that Santiago was still keeping Trip prisoner; that gave him no choice but to open the door.

Instantly he found he had been only half right. A hooded man was tied to a chair, but the prisoner was older and scrawnier than Trip had been.

The creaking of the door made the prisoner cringe, which made Oliver's next decision an easy one. He hurried across the room and when he dragged the sack away he was surprised to find Vaughan Price, the ostler from Prudence, looking at him with pained eyes above the gag.

Oliver offered a warming smile and reached out to remove the gag, but Vaughan jerked away and it took him several attempts to peel the gag from his mouth.

'I'm not here to cause you no trouble, Vaughan,' Oliver said.

'That's what Santiago claimed,' Vaughan said, concern making his voice high-pitched. 'So stop playing games, Erebus. I won't change my story. I told Santiago the truth.'

Oliver raised an eyebrow. 'You reckon I'm Erebus Finch?'

Vaughan looked him over, considering Oliver's incredulous expression. His eyes softened and he sighed with relief.

'Santiago promised me that Erebus would be the next man to come through the door.'

'I'm not Erebus. I'm Oliver Kincaid.'

Vaughan thought for a moment. 'Trip's brother?'

'Sure. What are you doing here?'

'That's what Santiago wanted to know. He didn't like my answer.'

Vaughan glanced at his bound arms and, getting the hint, Oliver put his hands to the ropes.

'What was that answer?' Oliver asked as he worked.

'Apparently anyone who shows an interest in that subject ends up dead, so it'd be best not to ask.'

Oliver winced. 'So you came for the dead men's gold too?'

Like Oliver, Vaughan winced, but he didn't reply until Oliver had loosened his bonds.

'Santiago told me he wasn't interested in it, but I didn't believe him.' Vaughan rubbed his legs, then he stood up. He stayed hunched over while prodding his ribs and stamping his feet to encourage circulation. 'Either way, I have to get away while I still can.'

'Most people are celebrating in the Queen of Spades tonight, but the ravine will be guarded again.' Oliver regarded Vaughan while rubbing his jaw. 'I doubt you can sneak out, and it'll be even harder with the gold.'

Vaughan smiled for the first time. 'And is a share of the gold the price of your help?'

'I don't care about the gold. I may be too late to help Trip, but I can still help you, and we have a common enemy in Santiago.'

Oliver waited until Vaughan nodded. Then he slapped his back and pointed at the door.

They hurried into the other room where Vaughan stopped to size up the equipment. His brow remained furrowed until with a shake of the head he appeared to dismiss the matter. At the main door Oliver peered round it and, as he saw nobody, they slipped outside.

Aside from the saloon and stable, the other buildings were in darkness. Adopting a casual gait, they walked away from the saloon until they reached the well.

Their presence there wouldn't look suspicious; as it turned out Vaughan wasted no time in dunking his head in a bucket and drinking his fill. Then he sat on the wall while Oliver drew up another bucket of water, which he used to dab at a bruise on his cheek.

When Vaughan was ready to move on, they worked their way back along the other side of town in the shadows. As they approached the saloon Vaughan became agitated, but Oliver felt calm despite the danger he was willingly facing. When they reached the corner it was Vaughan who speeded up.

The light in the stable lit up Yohann Johanson, who was sitting by the door enjoying the night air. He beckoned Oliver in with a frown and then considered Vaughan with curiosity.

'I don't know you,' he said, 'and I know everyone in town.'

'But I know you,' Vaughan said. 'You once owned a stable in Eagle Pass, but I heard you left in a hurry.'

'Yeah, some money went missing and I got the blame.' Yohann looked Vaughan up and down until his eyes narrowed with recognition. He got up to welcome him with a rare smile. 'And you own the Prudence stable. What are you doing here?'

'Looking for a fast horse and passage out of here.'

Yohann flinched; his posture was no longer relaxed as he gave Vaughan the same horrified look he'd given Oliver when he admitted he'd come here to look for Trip.

'What did you go and say that for?'

'Because you're my only hope.'

Vaughan smiled. 'We ostlers have to stick together.'

Yohann looked from one man to the other; then, with a shrug, he moved to step past them, forcing Oliver to block his path.

'Get out of my way,' Yohann demanded. 'I'm checking with Santiago before I do anything.'

'Which will make things worse for you when I tell him you helped Vaughan escape.'

Yohann gulped, confirming that this hollow threat had sounded convincing.

'He won't believe you,' Yohann said without conviction. 'I'll take my chances.'

Yohann swayed to the right and again Oliver moved to intercept him, but this time Yohann was only feinting and he went left. Vaughan moved to chase after him, but Oliver shook his head.

'Then I wish you luck,' he called after Yohann, 'when I tell Santiago you know where the dead men's gold is.'

Yohann stomped to a halt and swung

round to face them.

'He'll know that's a lie.'

Oliver smiled and stamped his feet, showing he'd noticed how fast Yohann had stopped and that no matter what Yohann claimed now, this was a lie he wasn't prepared to risk him telling.

'I'm sure he'll accept that, eventually. But by then the stable will be looking for a new ostler.'

'All right,' Yohann murmured, lowering his head. 'I won't tell Santiago nothing, but I'm not helping him escape.'

'I'm not asking you to. Just hide him. I'll do the rest.'

Oliver nodded to Vaughan before turning his steps to the saloon. He took deep breaths to gather his confidence for what he had to do next and by the time he'd taken several paces Yohann was ushering Vaughan inside the stable.

By the time he reached the saloon no ideas had come about how he would help Vaughan. But he figured his first task would be to get behind the bar without fuss, so that when Santiago discovered Vaughan had gone, hopefully nobody would remember his absence.

That hope fled the moment he walked through the door. The excited chatter died down and all eyes turned to him.

'So you're telling me,' Santiago declared in the quiet saloon, 'that this fat bartender shot up Murtagh Grieve?'

'He sure did,' someone called, 'and we'll make him pay for that.'

11

'Murtagh gave me no choice,' Oliver said. 'I take paying bar bills very seriously.'

Gabriel uttered an appreciative laugh, but elsewhere Oliver's comment generated only surly glares, so he crossed the room, feeling as he had done earlier that as long as he reached the bar everything would be fine. This time when he slipped behind the bar, that didn't appear to be the case.

Everyone was glaring at him while Murtagh's surviving colleagues had stood up to face the bar. Only Gabriel's presence at the end of the bar appeared to be stopping them from advancing on him.

'Explain yourself,' Santiago said from the corner of the saloon. 'Why did you get involved in the gunfight?'

Oliver didn't think any answer would

satisfy these men, but thankfully he didn't need to find one as Wilhelmina spoke up.

'He saved my life,' she said. 'If he hadn't braved the gunfire, one of you gun-toting fools would have shot me.'

'You shouldn't have tried to warn Rex. Not that it helped the last thorn in my side.' Santiago looked at Gabriel and then at Wilhelmina and Oliver with obvious intent. 'Or *was* he the last?'

Wilhelmina set her hands on her hips. 'I did nothing when you burnt down my saloon and I did nothing when you shot up Rex. Now I tend bar for Priscilla. As long as you don't cause no trouble in here, what you do is no concern of mine.'

'I agree,' Oliver said before Santiago could retort, which made Santiago glare at him, although at least it took his attention away from Wilhelmina.

'I don't care about your opinion,' Santiago muttered. 'One day soon you'll pay for shooting up Murtagh.'

The declaration made the men who had lined up before the bar grunt with approval. Several of them moved closer, but Oliver faced them, finding that Santiago's threat had filled him with confidence as, for the first time, someone had thought him a man who was worth threatening.

When they stopped he wondered whether he or Gabriel had curbed their aggressive moves, but then Priscilla came in from the back room; clearly they had heard her approach. She wended her way through the tables to stand beside Gabriel.

'There's been enough bloodshed today,' she declared. 'What happened in the heat of the moment outside, stays outside.'

'I know your rule,' Santiago said. 'You've operated it since I came here and I've always respected it.'

Santiago licked his lips, leaving his mouth still open, suggesting he would provide a qualifier; the silence in the room suggested others expected him to do so, but he said nothing until Priscilla prompted him:

'And with Rex's death, will you continue to respect my rule?'

Santiago chuckled, as if he'd won a small battle in making her ask for that clarification.

'I'm sure we can forge an arrangement for our new situation.'

She narrowed her eyes, showing she'd noted his subtle wording. Gabriel must have noted the tenseness in her voice, for he moved a half-pace ahead of her.

'Our old arrangement,' she said, 'works fine for me.'

Santiago glanced at Gabriel before he turned his eyes upon Priscilla, and his subtle movement made Erebus stand up.

'I'm sure it does, but remind me: what do I get out of our arrangement?'

'You get a pleasant place to spend the evening.' She spread her hands. 'Those of us who can remember Helliton before you arrived know why this saloon has grown.'

Santiago spread his hands even more magnanimously.

'That's a good point. I'll concede the Queen of Spades has done well in providing hospitality in the past.'

'I didn't mean that. I mean this saloon has grown because you've eliminated everyone who's stood in your way. Now I'm one of the few people left who came here before you.'

Now it was Santiago's turn to narrow his eyes as he noted her subtle wording.

'Why should that concern me?'

She smiled sweetly, seemingly pleased to have moved their confrontation on to this point. Slowly she looked around the saloon as she ensured that everyone knew her reply was important.

In anticipation of Santiago not liking her answer, Gabriel settled his stance while Erebus moved away from his table. The tenseness in the room made Oliver pleased he'd learnt enough to know Priscilla was alluding to Santiago's having eliminated anyone who was

147

interested in the gold.

She finished her consideration of the saloon looking at Santiago, making both Erebus and Gabriel stand tall, but before Priscilla could reply a steady thumping started up.

Oliver glanced to the right to see that Wilhelmina was slapping a hand on the bar while in her other hand she held a six-shooter, her elbow planted firmly on the bar. Oliver recognized the gun as the one he'd thrown aside.

Everyone else in the room turned to her. Santiago was the last to react, although his reaction was the most animated when he saw she'd aimed the gun at him.

'I thought,' Santiago said, his voice gruff, 'you weren't concerned about what I've done.'

'I told the truth,' Wilhelmina said, her voice clear in the otherwise quiet saloon room. 'But now you're causing trouble in here and so I'm stopping you.'

Santiago raised his hands and turned to address everyone.

'I'm not armed. I'm not causing trouble.' Santiago lowered a hand to point at Priscilla. 'But your bartender is causing trouble. I believe this is a good test of your rule.'

Priscilla took a moment to reply, suggesting she was considering defying Santiago and forcing a resolution, but then she hunched her shoulders and waved at Wilhelmina.

'Put down the gun,' she said in a resigned tone. 'We're all friends here and Helliton's troubles stay outside this saloon.'

Wilhelmina's only reaction was to raise the gun slightly.

'I'd prefer to think,' Santiago said, 'Helliton's troubles are behind us.'

'As would I.' Priscilla matched Santiago's earlier raised hands gesture while turning full circle. 'The moment Wilhelmina puts down the gun the next drink will be on the house.'

The gesture evoked a subdued grunt of approval. Then, when with a sorry shake of the head Wilhelmina lowered her gun, a more enthusiastic cheer sounded and the customers moved for the bar.

As bustle and activity drove away the tense atmosphere Santiago returned to his chair without taking up Priscilla's offer, but others did. So for the next fifteen minutes Oliver dealt with the customers while Wilhelmina loitered in the background.

Only when Erebus sat down beside Santiago did Priscilla go behind the bar. Wilhelmina joined her while Gabriel stayed on the other side.

'You shouldn't have pulled a gun on Santiago,' Priscilla said quietly to Wilhelmina when the customers had been dealt with and nobody was close enough to hear her.

'He wanted a confrontation,' Wilhelmina said. 'With everyone set against you, it would have turned out badly.'

'Don't be so certain of that. It was the right time to clarify where we go from here and I accepted the risk, but you gave him a way out. Now I don't know when he'll move against me.'

'Then move against him first. If you wait for him you won't prevail. You have nothing and he controls the whole town now except for the Queen of Spades.'

Priscilla looked at Gabriel for guidance; he shrugged.

'You have two gun-toting bartenders,' he said with a smile. 'What more could you need?'

'For you to stay,' Priscilla said while Wilhelmina fixed him with her earnest gaze, suggesting that they both wondered where his loyalties lay.

As Oliver knew why Gabriel had come to Helliton he moved down the bar to avoid accidentally revealing his secret, but the challenge didn't appear to concern Gabriel.

'I'll deal with the situation in my own way. That'll help you out too by removing your problems. Trust me.'

Priscilla considered him before she patted his arm and started to move away, but Wilhelmina shook her head, her upper lip curled in contempt.

'You're another one of those fools, aren't you?' she murmured. 'You've come to Helliton to look for something you'll never find.'

'I'm no fool,' Gabriel said levelly. 'When I leave here, nobody will doubt that.'

'I've heard that boast a hundred times. I'm sure every bartender has too. And yet nobody has ever fulfilled it.'

Wilhelmina looked at Oliver for support, but Oliver shook his head.

'Trip was no fool,' he said. 'He was interested in the — '

'Enough!' Priscilla said. She turned back to them, her raised voice made the room go quiet. She continued in the same loud tone. 'No arguments tonight. I can't afford any more free drinks.'

Then, her outburst having ensured that they couldn't continue their debate, Priscilla worked her way around the room. Over the next few hours she spoke with everyone and laughed at anything anyone said, as she adopted her usual genial host demeanour.

For their part Oliver and Wilhelmina didn't get into her spirit of reconciliation. They stayed behind the bar and scowled at the customers. Gabriel leaned on the bar, quietly watching everyone.

As it turned out, despite the earlier problems, the evening passed without incident. Even so, Oliver didn't relax, as he knew the calmness couldn't last.

Long before midnight and earlier than the previous night, the customers started slipping away, although, as then, Santiago and Erebus were the last to leave. With a wink at Oliver to show he wasn't interested in what those men did Gabriel headed upstairs. Priscilla soon followed him.

As Santiago got ready to leave Wilhelmina stood tall and folded her arms, watching his every move, but he left without looking at her. She set her lips in a pout and hurled a towel to the floor.

'No matter what Priscilla says,' she muttered from the corner of her mouth, 'that man will be the next to get a reckoning.'

'He might not be the very next one,' Oliver said, as through the window he watched Santiago walk to his office.

He busied himself with wiping down the bar so he wouldn't have to explain and thankfully, she didn't ask him to. Presently Erebus came up to the bar. He withdrew the gold eagle from his pocket.

'I know who you are,' he said with a sly smile.

Oliver shrugged. 'I'm just a bartender.'

'Why would a bartender from Dirtwood follow me?'

Erebus raised an eyebrow, although his blank gaze didn't suggest that he expected an answer before he tossed the coin and caught it without looking. Then he made for the door, leaving Wilhelmina to cast Oliver a bemused look that he blanked.

When Oliver was again the last man left in the saloon room, he collected glasses. Although he tried not to, through the window he watched Erebus walk away.

Erebus had almost moved from view into the gloom when Santiago came hurtling out of his office. Oliver heard his wail of anguish as he hurled his hat to the ground.

Santiago swirled round looking up and down the town's main street. His angry movements showed he was wondering where Vaughan had gone and who had helped him escape.

By the time he faced the saloon, Oliver had extinguished the lights and taken sanctuary behind the bar. When he noted that Santiago didn't avert his gaze from the saloon he dropped down, moving slowly so he couldn't be seen, and crawled into his sleeping place beneath the bar.

12

Unlike on his first day in Helliton, at first light Oliver was awoken by bustle outside.

The previous night, although he had heard distant noises, he had resisted the temptation to look through the window and he had slept well.

Pleasingly, having taken decisive action and created this situation, for the first time since he'd decided to come to Helliton he hadn't been scared. Even if he couldn't see how yet, he was sure that defying Santiago would lead him to answers about Trip's fate.

When he looked outside he saw that Santiago was organizing a systematic search of the town, starting at the buildings furthest away from the saloon. Between the town and the ravine riders were patrolling, showing he had ensured Vaughan hadn't escaped before he worked out where he was hiding.

'What's Santiago doing now?' Gabriel said at his shoulder, making Oliver flinch, as he hadn't heard him arrive.

Oliver opened and closed his mouth before he found a suitable reply.

'Last night, before I went to sleep, he came out of his office and he looked mighty angry. I guess this is the result.'

Gabriel moved forward to look him in the eye.

'We've not known each other for long, but I know when you're being evasive. You know something about this.' When Oliver didn't reply, Gabriel shook his head. 'Trip went into that office and he was never seen again. If I were you, I'd have looked in there.'

'I'm not you.'

'We've already established you and I aren't that different, and you left the saloon last night.' Gabriel looked aloft as he pieced together the situation. He smiled and leaned closer. 'What did you find in there?'

Oliver tried to meet Gabriel's eye,

but when he failed he gave a resigned shrug.

'I found a who, not a what.' Oliver raised a hand when Gabriel started to ask the obvious question. 'Don't ask for more details, as the fewer people who know the better.'

Gabriel frowned. 'You're worried about how I'll react, which means the person you freed from Santiago's office is after the gold too.'

'Like you, he's confident he knows where it is, but Santiago's keeping a tight rein on who can leave.' Oliver pointed at the riders patrolling before the ravine. 'So for now he's in the same position as you: being trapped in here with a whole lot of gunmen.'

'I prefer to think they're trapped in here with me.' Gabriel chuckled. 'But I've finally pieced together where the gold is, so tell your friend to forget about the gold and to use any opportunity I create to get out of here.'

Oliver nodded, leaving Gabriel to take up his usual position at the bar. He sat there, hunched over, ignoring events outside while appearing to be deep in thought. As Oliver didn't dare risk going outside to make sure that Yohann had hidden Vaughan well, he tried to lose himself in his morning cleaning ritual.

Unfortunately, no matter how hard he tried he couldn't avoid looking through the window and monitoring Santiago's progress. He noted that, unlike yesterday, Santiago took control while Erebus stayed back as an observer.

Building by building the searchers worked their way closer. The aggrieved postures of the people they left in their wake showed they were being thorough.

Santiago glanced at the saloon frequently, showing he had already concluded where Vaughan had gone to ground, but that he was eliminating all other possibilities first. He'd reached the building opposite his office when Priscilla and the others stirred.

Priscilla didn't ask for an explanation

of Santiago's activities, which suggested that he had searched the town before. As she studiously avoided looking at him, a worrying thought hit Oliver.

He became even more anxious when Wilhelmina didn't register surprise upon seeing the search, and busied herself elsewhere. So he stopped cleaning and sought her out, finding her on her knees scrubbing the floor behind the bar, something he'd not seen her do before.

'You didn't ask what Santiago's doing,' he said, standing over her.

'What he does,' she said, scrubbing harder, 'doesn't interest me.'

He went to one knee and took her wrist, halting her movements.

'You proved last night you're interested in what he does, so I reckon what's happening outside reminded you of a similar situation.'

She made a half-hearted attempt to continue scrubbing, making Oliver tighten his grip. She sighed and her shoulders slumped.

'Santiago's only done this once before.' She gulped. 'It was a few days after he brought Trip back to Helliton.'

Oliver released her hand and raised himself. He watched the search while collecting his thoughts.

'You told me Trip died.'

'I didn't lie.' She shrugged. 'I don't know for sure that Santiago was looking for him.'

'But you don't know for sure that he wasn't?'

'I don't, but I'm sure Trip's dead. Nobody saw him again after he was taken into Santiago's office.' She got up and laid a hand on his arm. 'But I guess that doesn't exclude other possibilities.'

Oliver swirled round to face her. 'Such as him escaping?'

She bit her bottom lip, appearing guilty at having given him hope.

'The ravine is the only way out of Helliton and that's guarded.'

'Guards are human, and if Trip could talk his way in . . . ' Oliver trailed off as another thought hit him.

Yohann hadn't wanted to help him, but when he'd forced his hand, he had a plan to hide Vaughan. Despite being here for long enough to know Santiago would conduct a thorough search, he had looked confident.

Yohann had known about Trip too, even if he hadn't wanted to talk about him. With his mind whirling with possibilities, Oliver joined Priscilla in watching the search.

By the time he'd decided he wasn't being foolish in harbouring the hope that Trip had escaped from Santiago's office and that Yohann had hidden him, Santiago had deemed the latest building to be clear.

As Santiago moved on to Yohann's stable, Oliver returned to cleaning. Only Priscilla's murmured comments told him that the search was ongoing, but the longer Vaughan remained undiscovered the greater Oliver's hopes grew that Yohann had found him a good hiding-place.

Ten minutes passed before Priscilla

grunted in irritation. With a heavy heart Oliver put down his brush to see what had concerned her, but unlike Priscilla he couldn't help but smile when he saw that the search of the stable had revealed nothing.

While Yohann stood in the stable doorway with his hands on his hips projecting an image of a man who was annoyed at having been suspected, Santiago headed purposefully towards the saloon with four armed men flanking him.

Santiago looked content as he paced up to the door and came inside. For once he took the lead and left Erebus standing outside his office.

'You have an unwanted guest hiding in here,' he said to Priscilla without preamble. 'I'll find him and take him off your hands.'

'Who is he?' Priscilla asked.

'You don't know him. Stand aside while I search the saloon.'

'You know my rule: Helliton's troubles — '

'I know your rule and I'll follow it.' Santiago smiled. 'You can accompany me while I remove our mutual problem.'

'I will search my saloon. If I find someone hiding in here, I'll remove him. What you do with him then is your concern.'

Santiago rubbed his jaw, as if considering, although his smug expression didn't change, making Oliver assume he'd already decided how to react.

'Your offer is acceptable.' Santiago gave a short bow and Priscilla turned away, but she'd taken a single step when he continued: 'But I've searched everywhere else in town and this is the only place he can be, so find him.'

Priscilla didn't reply other than to gesture at Gabriel to join her, but for once Gabriel shook his head.

'I'm sure this missing person isn't dangerous,' he said. 'I'll stay here and entertain your guests.'

Priscilla paused before walking to the

stairs. Although she didn't request her help, Wilhelmina followed her. Santiago smiled as he watched them leave, but the moment they moved from view his expression became stern.

'How much longer,' Santiago said, 'will you hide behind her petticoats?'

Gabriel stayed hunched over at the bar. 'I'll leave when I choose to leave, which may be never, or it may be today.'

'I reckon it'll be the former.'

Gabriel glanced to either side to observe where Santiago's four gunmen were standing.

'That's because you intend to kill me, is it?'

'I respect Priscilla's rule, so while you hide in here you're safe.' Santiago snorted a confident laugh. 'But you won't leave Helliton.'

Gabriel nodded slowly as he turned to face Santiago.

'Even the dead can't escape from Helliton.' He gestured, indicating the canyon. 'Because you get Yohann

Johanson to throw their bodies down the pit that lies behind your office.'

Santiago narrowed his eyes. 'You haven't left the saloon. How do you know that?'

Gabriel didn't reply, and although Oliver didn't know why his answer had worried Santiago, Gabriel's confident smile showed he had expected Santiago to be concerned. The gunmen picked up Santiago's surprise as they edged forward, awaiting his instructions.

Years of seeing trouble erupt in saloons meant that Oliver could judge tense situations well. Even before Santiago reacted he could tell that this was the moment when he would break Priscilla's rule. As a bar towel was the only object that was close to hand, he did the only thing he could do to help Gabriel: he swept the towel at Santiago's face.

Santiago jerked away, his hand rising to bat the towel away. He failed and it wrapped around his face, but his spooked gunmen took this incident as their cue to act.

The two men nearest to Santiago scrambled for their guns while the other two moved quickly for cover behind tables.

The second group had made the right response as Gabriel had already anticipated that this encounter would turn bad by jerking his hand to his holster. His gun cleared leather in a moment as he twisted at the hip, his six-shooter rising to pick out the first gunman.

A deadly shot high in the chest felled the gunman before he could draw. Gabriel's second shot tore into the centre of the second gunman's chest, making the man blast out an involuntary gunshot from his half-drawn gun; it embedded itself in the base of the bar.

Oliver flinched, but unlike every other time trouble had erupted when he was behind the bar he didn't duck down. Instead, he ran for the end of the bar as Gabriel picked out one of the fleeing gunmen.

A gunshot hammered into the gunman's side; he stumbled and twisted before a second shot to the back made him fold over the table that he had been trying to reach. The table toppled over, sending the shot man tumbling and revealing to Oliver that the fourth gunman had taken refuge behind the table, but by then Oliver had grabbed the end of the bar.

While gunshots rattled, he swung towards Santiago, who had extricated himself from the towel and was now facing Gabriel. Oliver raised his arms and he slammed into Santiago's side; his weight and speed carried them both across the room.

Santiago sidestepped, but he didn't move fast enough; his feet became entangled and both men fell over. Santiago landed on his chest with a pained grunt that was cut off when Oliver landed on top of him.

On the clean floor both men went sliding along until they crashed into a table, upending it. It landed on top of them. When Oliver pushed the table aside, Santiago was still beneath him, so Oliver dragged his arm up his back while pressing his face into the floor.

He raised himself, but he needed to take no further action as the fourth gunman was lying on his back displaying a bloodied chest, while the other three were lying still on the floor. Gabriel was standing in the centre of the room regarding him with amusement.

'I'm fast on the draw,' he said, 'but you're faster with that towel.'

Oliver nodded. While Gabriel checked the shot men he examined Santiago. By the time he'd confirmed Santiago had hit his head on the table and he was out cold, Priscilla was hurrying down the stairs with Wilhelmina close behind.

When Priscilla saw Gabriel she stopped and put a hand to her chest in relief.

'How did this happen?' she asked.

Gabriel smiled. 'Santiago forced the

situation. Even so, I assume I'm now barred.'

'You're not, but Santiago is.' She appraised the gunmen and frowned. 'Did you take on Erebus too?'

'No,' Gabriel said with a wince. He looked towards the window.

When Oliver looked in the same direction he winced too. Erebus had been standing at the corner, but he was no longer visible.

13

'It's down there,' Yohann Johanson said.

Vaughan Price peered into the pit. He could see down for around fifty feet.

'This pit doesn't look that deep. I can't believe nobody's been down there before.' He sniffed. 'The smell can't put everyone off.'

They were standing in a hollow ten feet down from ground level. Before them was a circular pit that was twenty feet across and which had been covered by a wooden platform, which they'd shoved aside.

Ten feet below the edge of the pit was a small cave in which Vaughan had hidden in overnight until Yohann had lowered a rope down to him. As he'd spent a sleepless night fearing that if he slept he might roll over and accidentally fall, no matter what happened now, Vaughan had vowed he'd never hide in there again.

'The bodies I've thrown down there put off most people,' Yohann said, 'but the pit is a lot deeper than you can see. This was the original well, but the water was hard to reach. When they opened up the other well, this one dried up and nobody's been able to get all the way down and claim the gold the Helliton gang dropped down there.'

'Or at least not anyone who's lived to explain what they saw.'

'That's right.' Yohann contemplated the ropes they'd brought; they were so heavy that they'd struggled to carry them from the stable and around the back of the Queen of Spades. 'Even these might not be long enough.'

'How do we find out?'

Yohann chuckled. 'I'd wondered when you'd ask.'

Vaughan regarded Yohann's fixed smile and sighed.

'I assume going down is the price of my freedom?'

Yohann nodded. 'You get the gold

out of the pit, and I'll get you and the gold out of Hell Town.'

Vaughan fingered the end of the rope. He had hated lowering himself down the canyon side and he had hated even more clambering down to the cave. This was worse as he couldn't see the bottom and he couldn't gauge his chances of success.

Worst of all, it would probably take all his strength to get down, and then he would have to regather his strength to climb back up while somehow working out how to raise the gold, if it was down there.

'So you've planned for this . . . ' Vaughan trailed off as Yohann needlessly busied himself rearranging the rope into a neater pile. 'You have tried this before, and you failed.'

Yohann pointed down the hole. 'Just get down there before someone sees us. That gunfire means there's been another showdown and that gives us an opportunity, but the distraction won't last for ever.'

Vaughan stared at Yohann until Yohann returned his gaze.

'You have failed, but you didn't pay the price.' Vaughan waited, but Yohann didn't reply. 'How many men have you sent down there? How many have never come back up again?'

'You know the legend. They say the bones of a hundred men lie scattered around the dead men's gold.'

'So why do you think I'll defeat the curse?'

'More rope, fewer gunslingers.' Yohann waited for Vaughan to reply. When no reply came he continued: 'Five years ago, after I got blamed for that money going missing, I came here in search of the gold. Unlike the others who'd holed up here, I was no gunslinger. I'm just an ordinary man, like you are.'

'We're not that alike. I had no choice about coming here.'

Yohann shrugged. 'Either way, I worked hard and I bided my time. I earned everyone's trust by being useful

174

and by keeping my head down. Others searched and killed and died, but I avoided trouble. I figured out where the gold was, as others had, except unlike the others I showed no interest in it.'

'While you waited for the opportunity to claim it for yourself?'

'Sure. I'm one of the few men who can come and go through the ravine without question, because nobody's concerned about what harmless old Yohann Johanson does.' Yohann bent down to pick up the end of the rope. 'But there's one other thing that sets me apart from the rest: I'm honest. I'll share the gold with you, but you have to get it.'

Vaughan sighed. 'How can I trust you on that?'

Yohann held out the rope. 'You can't.'

*   *   *

'Santiago did a lot of things right,' Priscilla said, 'but he picked the wrong way to force a confrontation. Whoever he was looking for isn't hiding here.'

Gabriel glanced at Oliver, inviting him to explain, but Oliver ignored him and continued with the duty he'd allocated himself, of guarding Santiago. So far Santiago hadn't stirred.

'Santiago claimed to have looked everywhere,' Gabriel said. 'So either he missed him or . . . '

Gabriel turned to Oliver. Although Oliver again ignored the opportunity to explain, he walked across the room to stand over Santiago.

'He's still out cold,' Oliver said. 'But I'm sure he'll be able to answer your questions soon.'

'I'd prefer my good friend to answer them.'

Oliver took a deep breath. 'The missing man is Vaughan Price. He appeared to know — '

'Vaughan!' Gabriel looked aloft. 'He told me where the gold was. He got it wrong, but . . . '

He hurried to the side of the window

and peered at the nearby buildings. Nobody was about, so he pressed his cheek to the wall to look towards the canyon side.

'Forget about the gold,' Priscilla said. 'We have Santiago and once Erebus's been dealt with, we'll all be safe.'

'I came here for the gold and I'll leave here with it.' Gabriel turned from the window. 'But that doesn't mean I have to leave without you. Come with me.'

'I'm pleased you've asked me that at last, but . . . ' She sighed and shook her head. 'My life is here. I'm not abandoning my saloon on the eve of this town's finally being tamed.'

'A town like this can never be tamed. Either more outlaws will come seeking to hole up away from the law, or this place will die.'

'I'll take . . . ' The words stuck in her throat, forcing her to cough. 'I'll take my chances.'

Gabriel gazed at her until she turned away and joined Wilhelmina.

'As will I,' he said to her back.

Gabriel gnawed at his bottom lip until with a nod he appeared to make a decision. He hurried over to Santiago and raised his head from the floor.

Santiago's head lolled and even when Gabriel had deposited him on a chair, he couldn't keep himself upright.

'While he's in this state,' Oliver said, 'he won't be able to help you.'

'This is the ideal state for him to help me.'

Gabriel didn't explain other than to direct a confident wink at Oliver. Then he raised Santiago to his feet and walked him around in a circle.

At first, Santiago didn't help him, but after Gabriel had walked him around several times he started murmuring and trying to shake Gabriel off. That reaction was good enough for Gabriel and he took him to the door, where Gabriel craned his neck to appraise the situation.

'Good luck,' Oliver said.

'Obliged, and remember: I don't

need no more heroics from you. Stay here and don't come out until I've dealt with Erebus.'

Gabriel waited until Oliver nodded, then he looked at Priscilla, but she was making herself busy with Wilhelmina behind the bar in a stilted manner that made it clear she was ignoring him. So Gabriel kicked open the door and holding Santiago before him he edged outside sideways.

As he walked past the window it was clear that with every step Santiago was becoming more aware of what was happening; he held his head up and he walked with more assurance.

When they'd passed the window they progressed diagonally across the main drag towards Santiago's office. They were the only people Oliver could see outside and although Gabriel was in a better position to notice trouble, Oliver still looked out for Erebus.

'Which way did he go?' Priscilla asked in a level tone that suggested she already knew the answer.

'He's heading to Santiago's office.' Oliver watched Gabriel move on for a few paces. 'Although he appears to be making for the back. Perhaps there's another way in there.'

'There isn't.'

Oliver turned from the window. 'You know where he's going.'

Priscilla sighed. 'Everyone goes there in the end, one way or the other.'

She glanced at Wilhelmina, who shook her head and completed the thought.

'So far it's always been the other.'

'Are you saying you know where the gold is too?'

'We'd never admit that,' Wilhelmina said with a shrug. 'Saying that has always been fatal, and no matter what happens to Santiago now, I reckon it always will be.'

'If you know where it is, surely Santiago knows too.' Oliver pondered for a moment. 'So why doesn't he just take it and leave?'

Priscilla raised a hand to try to stop

him speaking and when he did stop, she shook her head.

'Forget you ever had that thought.'

'I can't when I still have a mystery to solve. Who else knows?' Oliver waited, but neither woman replied, so he slapped the wall. 'Why won't you answer my questions?'

Priscilla turned her back on him, but Wilhelmina flashed a smile.

'Because we're saving your life. Everyone figures it out in the end. It's not difficult. That's why so many people get to hear about it and why they come here and why they die.'

'If it's such common knowledge, why does mentioning the gold anger Santiago?'

'He's trying to stem the tide until he can claim it for himself, but that's as futile as trying to stick a cork back in a shaken barrel of beer.'

'And I assume you won't explain what that means?' When both women said nothing, he shrugged. 'Then I'll get my own answers.'

He went back behind the bar and found the six-shooter he'd claimed from Rex yesterday. He figured he'd be more effective with a gun he'd used before, albeit unsuccessfully, and sure enough the weight felt more comfortable in his grip than it had done before.

He still didn't like being armed, so to avoid holding the weapon he took a holster from one of the dead gunmen. Priscilla and Wilhelmina watched him, shaking their heads, but he shuffled the holster into a position where his bulging stomach wouldn't impede his drawing the weapon, and turned away.

When he reached the door his heart was thudding, but not as badly as yesterday. He sidestepped outside and pressed his back to the wall, trying to make himself as small as possible while looking at every part of town at the same time.

He saw nobody other than Gabriel, who swung his gun towards him before he registered who he was. Gabriel nodded his thanks before he moved on and that gave Oliver the confidence to peel himself away from the wall.

He walked sideways past the window and along the front of the saloon while darting his head from side to side as he looked where Gabriel wasn't looking. To his delight, Gabriel nodded at the end of the saloon, silently conveying that he couldn't see past the saloon and Oliver should check out the blind side of the wall first.

Gabriel's trust made him walk with more assurance, and Oliver drew his six-shooter and hurried to the corner, where he stopped. He heard nothing, so with his gun thrust out he edged closer while mentally rehearsing the motion of darting forward and back quickly.

He was settling his weight on his toes, ready to spring forward, when pain shot up his arm and the gun was dashed from his hand. A cry of surprise escaped his lips as in a blur of motion a hand appeared around the corner and grabbed his wrist.

By the time his senses had caught up

with what was happening, he'd been swung around and was being held from behind with a firm arm constricting his neck and a gun jabbed into his back.

He gulped when he worked out that Erebus had been hiding beyond the corner and was now holding him, but by then he could do nothing other than direct an apologetic shrug at Gabriel. While Gabriel turned Santiago to face them, Erebus walked Oliver away from the wall.

'Stand-off,' Erebus called as he stopped ten paces from Gabriel.

'It was always going to come to this,' Gabriel said. 'But we don't need others to sort out our differences.'

'We're alike.' Erebus chuckled as he drew the gun out from behind Oliver to hold it at his side.

'We are, but you shot up my friend Newton Clay.'

'Not the gold, then?' Erebus transferred his weight as he loosened his grip around Oliver's neck.

'I don't have to explain nothing to

you. Let Oliver go and I'll let Santiago go. Then we'll end this.'

For long moments Erebus didn't react, making Santiago speak up for the first time, although his voice was weak and his half-closed eyes suggested he wasn't fully aware of the situation.

'Gabriel's no match for you,' he murmured. 'Do it, Erebus.'

Erebus tensed and Oliver edged forward as he tested whether he'd been released. Although he hadn't, to his surprise Erebus fired. His gunshot sliced into Santiago's chest making him arch his back and bump into Gabriel, knocking his right arm aside as he swung his gun up.

Santiago fell to his knees, but Gabriel was still trying to free his arm when Erebus fired over Santiago's right shoulder. The shot caught Gabriel low in the chest, making him stumble so that the two wounded men swung away from each other.

A second shot to the heart downed Gabriel. He lay for a moment while struggling to rise, but he failed and flopped down to lie on his back, breathing shallowly.

Erebus contemptuously shoved Oliver aside, making him go sprawling on his knees before he moved on to stand over Santiago, who looked up at him with eyes that were already blank. Erebus watched him until he was sure he'd breathed his last, then he moved on to Gabriel.

'He talked too much,' Erebus said simply.

Gabriel opened and closed his mouth several times without making a sound until he formed a single word.

'Why?' he breathed.

Erebus knelt down in a position where Gabriel could see what he was doing. Then he withdrew the gold eagle from his pocket and tossed it in the air.

When he'd caught the coin on the back of his hand, Gabriel nodded, then his head lolled to one side. Erebus watched him, then got up to face Oliver.

'So,' Oliver said with a sigh, 'you too.'

14

'We all want the gold,' Erebus said.

'I don't,' Oliver said.

Erebus snorted in disbelief. 'Because you're just a bartender?'

Oliver looked at the gold coin, and the final piece of his theory about what had happened to Trip slipped into place.

'I'm surprised you haven't worked out why I'm here yet. I'm Oliver Kincaid, Trip's brother.'

'And?'

Oliver had expected Erebus to shoot him after he'd killed Gabriel, but since Erebus seemed to be delaying, Oliver saw no reason not to get the satisfaction of confirming what he now suspected.

'Eighteen months ago in a poker game in the Queen of Hearts, Trip won a coin from the dead men's gold.

Santiago dragged him back here and kept him prisoner. Trip was never seen again, but he was a resourceful man. I reckon he escaped, but then you found him and stole the coin.'

Oliver nodded at Erebus's coin and, getting his meaning, Erebus tossed it while licking his lips.

'I found this ten years ago.'

Oliver's shoulders slumped. He felt more disappointed about his theory unravelling than alarmed at his dire predicament. When Erebus saw his reaction, he sighted him down the barrel of his gun.

With a hopeless feeling making his guts rumble, Oliver got to his feet, determined that, if nothing else, he would face the end standing up.

'I'm pleased to hear that,' he said. 'It means Trip escaped, after all.'

Erebus shook his head and tensed, but he didn't fire while his expression-less gaze suggested he was thinking. Then he narrowed his eyes and gestured, indicating the whole canyon.

'Vaughan's missing. He wants the gold too.'

'As you said, they all do.'

'Santiago suspected you, but who helped you?'

'The same man who helped Trip escape, except when Trip got away from here, he'd have left with the gold. That means you and all the rest have wasted your lives over nothing.'

Erebus paced towards him, making Oliver tense in supposition of that being his final defiant statement, but instead Erebus turned him around and shoved his shoulder.

'Take me to Vaughan.'

Oliver dug in a heel and swirled round to face Erebus.

'I can't do that. Vaughan's long gone.'

'He's still here.' Erebus waited but Oliver said nothing. 'Maybe Wilhelmina and — '

'They know nothing,' Oliver snapped.

Erebus met his gaze and, concerned that his outburst had proved he didn't want Erebus questioning the women,

Oliver looked past him at the space behind Santiago's office. Erebus noted where he was looking with a knowing smile and grabbed his arm.

'We'll start at the pit.'

In relief that Erebus wouldn't question the women, Oliver let Erebus lead him on. They had passed Santiago's office when a gasp escaped his lips as a sudden thought hit him that was so shocking he stopped in his tracks.

'The smell's getting bad,' Oliver said, hoping to cover his mistake.

Erebus tugged his arm, dragging him on, glaring at him with irritation.

'That's because the legend's true.'

Oliver gulped. 'If the gold is lying at the bottom of the pit, why do you think you can claim it when so many others have failed?'

'Santiago was a clever man.'

Erebus said no more as the hollow which, Oliver assumed, contained the pit was ahead. As Oliver figured that the only reason for Erebus keeping him alive was that he thought him useful, he hazarded a guess at what his plan might be.

'I assume the pit is too deep for anyone to reach the bottom, but once Hell Town calms down, you can organize a proper search. The equipment in Santiago's office means he had a plan to erect platforms and ladders to get down — '

'Silence,' Erebus muttered. He stopped to glare at Oliver and then pushed him on, making him walk in the lead.

As more of the hollow became visible, Oliver craned his neck. His upper lip had already curled back in anticipation of what he would see, but when he saw the circular hole in the hollow, he accepted that he wouldn't be faced with a horrific scene.

A few paces on, on the near side of the pit, he saw Yohann and Vaughan kneeling down.

The two men saw him coming, so Oliver did the only thing he could do to warn them by raising his hands in a warding-off gesture. The men looked at him in puzzlement until their expressions turned to shock when they saw that Erebus was following him.

Erebus grabbed Oliver's shoulder and jabbed his gun into his back, letting him know what would happen if Vaughan and Yohann fought back. When they reached the edge of the hollow, Erebus appraised the coils of rope lying beside the men with a smirk.

'Carry on,' he said in a forced, light tone and gesturing at the pit with his gun.

The two men sighed before they played out the ropes, although they worked slowly. For his part, Erebus moved a few paces away from Oliver, to where he could watch him as well as the other men.

Yohann secured one end of a rope to a post supporting the platform, which they had pushed aside to reveal the pit. Then he lowered the other end down into the pit.

When he'd played out all the rope

Yohann moved to tie an end around Vaughan's waist, but Vaughan shook his head.

'You know more than I do about the pit,' Vaughan said. 'You go down.'

'But you're younger and fitter,' Yohann said. 'And I'm afraid of heights.'

'That's no excuse for what you've done.'

The two men glared at each other until in mounting anger Erebus grunted and loosed off a gunshot. Yohann flinched and looked at his arm to find the shot had frayed his sleeve.

'Decide, now!' Erebus said.

Without even looking at Yohann Vaughan wrapped the end of the second rope around his waist and moved to the edge, while Yohann held the other end to support him in case he fell.

For the first time they were working efficiently. Within moments Vaughan was lowering himself over the edge while Yohann watched anxiously.

Erebus didn't relax, and when Vaughan had disappeared from view Oliver saw the reason why. Wilhelmina and Priscilla had come out of the saloon and were kneeling on either side of Gabriel's body.

They got to their feet and came towards the pit with determined paces, causing Erebus to check Yohann was occupied down in the hollow before he swung round to face them. As usual, he didn't look at Oliver, appearing to dismiss him as a threat.

'You killed Gabriel,' Priscilla said when she was twenty paces away.

'And Santiago,' Erebus said in a light tone. 'Be grateful.'

'I'm not.' Priscilla stopped five paces from Erebus with Wilhelmina at her shoulder. 'Helliton belongs to the people who care about the town. Those whose greed for the gold lures them down into the pit are always doomed. You're no different.'

'Don't threaten me.'

'I wasn't. The gold's cursed. My

husband threw it down there before he got shot to hell. His last words were a promise that if he couldn't have it, nobody would.'

Erebus snorted a laugh. 'There's no curse.'

'I've been here since the beginning. I've seen enough to know that the curse is real. Men go into the pit. They don't come out.' She peered past Erebus at Yohann. 'Ask him. He's been here for longer than most and you'll never get him to go down there.'

Erebus shook his head, but when Wilhelmina shrieked and Priscilla jerked forward with a hand rising to her mouth, he swirled round to look at what had alarmed them.

Oliver turned too, and saw that Yohann had fallen on to his chest and was no longer holding the rope. Only when Vaughan's desperate and distant cry of distress sounded from the pit did Oliver work out what had happened.

Yohann had tripped over the post securing Vaughan's rope. Both ropes had been shaken free and now they were snaking over the edge with a speed that showed Vaughan was falling uncontrollably.

Oliver stepped forward, but before he found a route down into the hollow the ends of both ropes flipped over the edge. For long moments everyone remained still, but Vaughan didn't make another sound.

Yohann edged forward to peer into the pit and then looked up at them while shaking his head.

'He's gone,' he said simply.

'The curse,' Priscilla said with a sad but triumphant tone in her voice that made Erebus wave a dismissive hand at her.

'He just fell,' he muttered.

'As did all the others.' Priscilla sniffed to reinforce her point.

'There is no curse. There *is* no curse!'

Erebus's words echoed back at him from the canyon walls. Priscilla turned to Wilhelmina and both women smiled knowingly. Erebus's face reddened as he lost his usual calm.

'Curse or no curse,' Yohann called, 'I'm not fetching more rope.'

Erebus stepped down into the hollow, his gun jerking up to point at Yohann, who stared defiantly up at him. Erebus fired into the ground at Yohann's feet making him raise a boot and step to one side, but when he settled his stance, he folded his arms.

'Go,' Erebus muttered.

Erebus fired again, this time nicking Yohann's forearm. Yohann clapped a hand to the wound. He winced from the pain and glanced at his bloody hand, but he still shook his head.

'The dead men's gold is cursed. Somebody else can prove it isn't.'

Erebus stopped halfway down the slope and levelled his gun at Yohann's chest, but Yohann glared up at him. Oliver gulped when he foresaw the direction this confrontation would take.

Erebus would force someone to go into the pit, and he, Oliver, would be the next choice.

Oliver doubted he'd be able to support his own weight on the perilous descent, never mind defeat a curse that at this moment felt real. Erebus had his back to him, and as he was no longer acting in a controlled manner Oliver moved towards him.

Erebus gave no sign that he'd heard him, so Oliver advanced another pace and then another. The dirt on the slope was loose and he walked cautiously, but he figured Erebus would notice him soon, and when Yohann muttered about the curse again he broke into a run.

He pounded down the slope, expecting with every pace that Erebus would turn and shoot him, but Erebus was concentrating on Yohann. Oliver got to within three paces of him before Erebus flinched and swirled round to face him.

Oliver ducked, expecting swift retribution, and as he was already leaning forward the motion unbalanced him.

His right foot slipped, pitching him forward on to his left knee. He slid down the slope with his arms wheeling until he barrelled into Erebus's legs. Both men went down.

In a swirl of entwined arms and legs they rolled down the slope. The sky appeared to Oliver to spin around him five times before he slammed down on his back.

He shook himself and groggily raised his head, to find that Erebus had rolled further on for several yards; he too was stirring. Yohann stared at them both in horror until he looked to the right and then rocked back and forth on his toes in apparent indecision.

Oliver raised himself and saw that Yohann was looking at Erebus's gun, which had been shaken free when he'd tumbled down the slope. Before Yohann could make up his mind whether to risk running for it, Oliver rolled to his feet and hurried to the gun.

On the run he scooped it up and ran on for six paces before he turned to face Erebus, who was still getting up slowly. When Erebus was on his feet Oliver regarded him with disdain.

'Yesterday you nearly missed a man from two feet away.' Erebus spread his hands, chuckling, inviting Oliver to take a shot at him. 'I'm in no danger from a useless bartender.'

'You got that wrong.' Oliver waited until Erebus sneered before explaining. 'Yesterday I *actually* missed a man from two feet away. Gabriel shot him.'

Erebus threw back his head and roared with laughter. He moved forward with his right hand held out to claim the gun. Oliver reckoned Erebus was right to be confident; he gave a resigned sigh while his shoulders slumped.

Then he fired.

From five paces away he was as inaccurate as he had been yesterday. The gunshot slewed two feet wide of its target and all it achieved was to make Erebus glare at him in anger for having dared to take a shot at him.

With only a moment to act, Oliver realized for the first time some of the things he'd been doing wrong, such as moving his arm and closing his eyes as he fired.

He backed away, stiffened his arm and fired again.

He still closed his eyes at the crucial moment, but this time firing somehow felt different, although he couldn't work out why until Erebus stumbled with a hand rising to clutch his bloodied chest.

He met Erebus's eyes. Erebus looked at him with surprise and perhaps respect. Then Erebus pitched forward to land face down in the dirt.

'And I'm not a useless bartender,' Oliver said. He threw the gun on to Erebus's motionless back. 'I'm a very good bartender.'

15

Oliver looked down into the pit, listening to Erebus's progress as he crunched against the sides of the pit. The sounds became ever fainter until he couldn't hear anything more. He didn't hear Erebus hit the bottom.

He nodded to Yohann, who had batted his hands together after tipping Erebus over the edge, and moved around the pit seeking a different angle. He saw only darkness below, so he settled down as close to the edge as he dared.

'Vaughan,' he called. 'Can you hear me?'

He heard only his cry echoing back at him. He tried again, but as the dark pit seemed to draw him forward, making him feel as if he were in danger of toppling into its depths, he moved away.

'Nobody has ever come out there

alive,' Priscilla said from the top of the hollow, 'and I heard Vaughan fall for a great distance.'

'I know, but he deserved a better fate than all the others who have gone down there never to return.'

Yohann nodded and patted his back.

'As we all claimed,' he said, 'the gold is cursed. I'd never go down there, but I'll have nothing but admiration for the first man to go down and come out again.'

'Someone may already have done that.' Oliver recalled the ropes that Yohann and Vaughan had used and tried to work out how far they would have reached. 'It's possible someone could have lowered themselves to the bottom and then climbed out with the gold. After all, you thought it was possible.'

Yohann dismissed this possibility with a vigorous shake of his head.

'It's still down there,' he murmured, seemingly talking to himself. 'It has to be.'

As Oliver didn't care about the fate of the gold, he turned away, leaving it to people who did care, but then a troubling thought hit him. He turned back.

'You brought two ropes because you thought that would be enough. But you've never been down there, so how do you know there's a place to stand to use the second rope?'

Yohann didn't meet his eye, but turned away from the pit, obviously attempting to ignore the question. Oliver hurried to bar his way. Yohann looked past him, seeking a way out of the hollow, but Wilhelmina and Priscilla stood at the top with their arms folded, showing they wouldn't let him out until he'd answered Oliver's question.

'I've been here for five years,' Yohann said, shaking his head. 'I've seen the equipment Santiago brought and I worked out how he planned to build platforms and ladders to get down there. I'd always hoped to use a simpler method.'

'Who else?' Oliver glared at Yohann, but when Yohann put on a blank expression which to Oliver's eyes looked guilty, he prompted: 'Who else has been down there?'

Yohann gulped. 'I can't remember all their names.'

'All? So you recruited lots of people to risk their lives while you stayed safe up here?'

'Stop accusing me. When you came to me, I defied Santiago and helped Vaughan.'

'You only helped him so he could help you, just like you did eighteen months ago when another escaped prisoner came to you for help.'

Oliver advanced on Yohann, who tried to hurry out of the hollow, but his feet slipped. He fell on to his chest and slid down to the base. He twisted over quickly, to find Oliver standing over him.

'Get away from me,' Yohann said, glaring up at him while shifting backwards on his rump, moving his feet frantically.

'Admit it,' Oliver said while advancing on him with deliberate paces as Yohann moved closer to the pit. 'You hid Trip.'

Yohann stopped feet from the edge and ventured a smile.

'I helped your brother. Without me, Santiago would have found him and killed him.'

'I'd have believed you if you'd told me that straight away instead of only admitting it now that I'm threatening you.'

After this revelation Yohann sat up straight, appearing to gather confidence.

'You're no threat.' Yohann got to his feet and gestured at him. 'Like Erebus said, you're just some bartender who hid behind a gunslinger, except that the gunslinger got shot up.'

'I killed Erebus, and that means I'm a man you'll respect.' Oliver waited, but Yohann didn't reply. 'Even if you won't tell me everything, you'll never defeat the curse. After you sent Trip down there, he got out and took the gold with him.'

Yohann's eyes glazed, suggesting this was possible before he got over his irritation by angrily advancing on him.

'He didn't. Trip was as greedy as the rest, and like the rest he defied the curse and got himself killed.'

Oliver appeared to concede his point with a shrug, making Yohann flash a triumphant smile before he used all his pent-up rage of the last few days to aim a swiping blow at Yohann's face. Buoyed up by his success with Erebus, the punch connected with Yohann's nose with a satisfying crunch, making him jerk his head back.

As Yohann threw his hands to his bloodied nose and the two women murmured with surprise, Oliver followed through with a second blow, aimed at Yohann's cheek.

This blow wasn't as well-aimed as the first one, and it caught his opponent only a glancing blow to the chin, but it still made him twist round. A third blow flattened Yohann's ear, causing him to stumble while Oliver rubbed his stinging hand against the palm of the other.

The pain made Oliver unwilling to hit Yohann again, so he roared and bundled him away. Yohann teetered, then disappeared from view.

Oliver blinked in surprise as he saw that they'd moved nearer to the pit than he'd thought, and he'd knocked Yohann over the edge. He inched forward until he saw Yohann dangling below the rim with a hand grasping the post he'd knocked over earlier when he'd released Vaughan.

'The truth.' Oliver thrust out his left hand, but then he drew it away. 'Now!'

'I didn't kill Trip,' Yohann babbled. 'I didn't. He went into the pit and he found a ledge. It was his idea for me to throw down a second rope. He thought he could reach the bottom with it.'

'And did he?'

Yohann glanced at Oliver's hand held

inches from his own. In encouragement, Oliver planted a foot against the post and rocked it making Yohann jerk down.

'I don't know. We made too much noise and someone came to investigate. It was dark, but I had to leave him. When I came back the next morning, the rope was no longer hanging over the edge and Trip didn't reply when I shouted down.'

'So he got out?'

'He couldn't have done!' Yohann shouted as Oliver pushed the post and made him jerk down again. 'There's no way out of town. Someone must have dislodged the rope. Whoever did that killed him, not me.'

'So a whole lot of men's last moments were spent dangling over this abyss knowing you were the only man who could save them?'

When Yohann nodded, Oliver kicked the post, making it slip out of the dirt. Yohann hurtled away into the pit.

Yohann shrieked, but before he fell

silent Oliver had turned to make his way out of the hollow. Wilhelmina and Priscilla held out hands to help him back to ground level, where he looked past them at Gabriel's body.

He still felt as numb as he had felt after he'd shot Erebus, but both women looked at him, murmuring sympathetically.

'You did the right thing,' Wilhelmina said.

'I didn't,' Oliver murmured. 'I killed and what I feared is true. It gets easier.'

'Perhaps it does, but what sets you apart from the other men who come here is you're a bartender, not a killer, and you can stop.'

'And despite the curse,' Priscilla said when Oliver nodded reluctantly, 'one day we'll find out what's at the bottom of the pit.'

'I already know what's down there,' Oliver said. 'It's the bones of the hundred men who have died trying to claim the dead men's gold, but the gold's not there because Trip escaped with it.'

The women cast sceptical glances at each other, but Oliver pretended he hadn't seen. He moved past them.

'After what you've done, you have a job for as long as you want it. You could have a good life here now that Erebus has actually cleaned up Helliton.'

'Except I got the answer I came here to find. Now I'm leaving.' Oliver looked across to the wreckage of the burnt-out Queen of Hearts. 'I have a life outside of Hell Tow — Helliton, and I have a saloon of my own to run.'

'I didn't know that.' Priscilla smiled. 'In that case, I'll speak to the guards in the ravine. They'll let you pass.'

She walked away, but Wilhelmina stayed.

'I didn't know you owned a saloon either,' she said.

'Admittedly it's in a bad state at the moment.'

'As bad as my saloon?'

'Worse, but I can spruce it up.'

Wilhelmina laughed and with a smile on her lips, she walked towards the wreckage of her own saloon. She rooted around until she found what she was looking for, which turned out to be a bar towel.

'If you're going to be cleaning up, you'll need this.' She held out the towel, but Oliver didn't move. 'Take it. Then a part of my life in Helliton can leave with you.'

'No,' Oliver said. 'Bring it.'

* * *

'Leave me alone,' Yohann murmured, his voice as ragged as his breath. 'Let me die in peace.'

'You will die if you don't move,' Vaughan said.

'But I can't move. I'm all broken up.'

Yohann fixed Vaughan with his pained gaze, his eyes watery in the poor light making Vaughan turn away to consider their predicament. He moved awkwardly as, like Yohann, he could sum up his own condition as being broken up.

He couldn't move his numb right arm and he'd vomited when he'd made the mistake of looking at his shattered left leg. Yohann was in a worse state, but then, he'd not enjoyed the dubious advantage of a relatively soft landing.

Vaughan was unsure how far he had fallen, but it had been a long and terrifying descent into the unknown. After the rope had come loose, he had fallen on to an outcrop where he had been trying groggily to regain his senses when Yohann had come sliding down and knocked him off the ledge.

As Yohann tumbled along below him, he had slid down a narrow chimney in the rock despite his attempts to check his fall by pressing his body to the rock wall of the chimney. Then the slope had grown steeper and his descent had become impossible to control.

He had fallen for two rapid heart-beats, hit another ledge, clung on for a moment, then he'd slid down a vertical spiralling tunnel until he'd emerged into clear space. This time he had counted three frantic heartbeats without hitting anything.

His only hint of what lay below was Yohann's shriek of terror, which had cut off abruptly, so he'd tensed for a moment before he hit the surprisingly soft bottom of the pit.

He had lain in the dark wondering how he could have survived such a long fall. It was only when his returning senses granted him the unwelcome gift of smell that the rank, rotting odour invaded his nostrils and gave him the answer.

He was lying buried in a heap of the bodies that had been thrown down here.

With two broken limbs and the other two barely working it'd taken him a long and hellish time to fight his way out of the mound of decaying corpses. Now he lay beside the dying Yohann and he couldn't help but think Yohann was the lucky one.

The thin stream of light filtering in from above enabled him to see the walls that surrounded him, confirming there was no way out.

Scattered heaps showed that the bottom was fifty feet across. Some of the heaps were rocks, but most of them were bodies ranging from bones wrapped in rags to the men who had been killed in yesterday's gunfight.

As the bodies lay across the whole area, Vaughan surmised that some men had survived the fall and they'd spent their last moments dragging themselves away from the central pile. Vaughan's only aim was to find an area where the smell was bearable, so he dragged himself on.

He had just found an area where there was only rock beneath him when his eyes became accustomed enough to the gloom to see an angular shape. Glumly he peered at it; the dull hints of pain that were penetrating the numbness, along with his awareness of his hopeless situation, were destroying any interest he had in his surroundings.

Then he realized what he was seeing.

Twenty feet ahead lay a strongbox. He even mustered a smile when he discerned the shapes of the bodies lying to either side of it.

'I've found it,' he said. He waited, but Yohann didn't respond. 'The dead men's gold is down here, after all!'

'Tell me what it looks like,' Yohann said, his voice almost too low to hear.

'It's in a strongbox.' Vaughan uttered a hollow laugh that echoed back at him. 'And like the legend says, the bones of a hundred men are lying around it.'

'Including mine.' Yohann laughed, but the effort made him cough and then murmur in pain. 'The curse still beat us.'

While he still had the strength to enjoy the sight, Vaughan dragged himself along. He covered half the distance quickly, but before long every time he put a hand to the ground, he pressed down on objects that were wet and yielding or which cracked and shifted, and so he struggled to move.

He had to claw bones and the softer

objects aside to get purchase on the hard ground, and he had lost any sense of how far he had moved when his leading shoulder crunched against the strongbox.

'I've reached it,' he called. 'We've beaten the curse.'

Yohann didn't reply and so he levered himself up to a sitting position. Resting his back against the strongbox, he tried to pick out Yohann from amongst the bodies, but he couldn't see him.

He turned to the box. With his one working hand he pushed a body off the lid and then set about finding out how to open it, but he didn't need to as removing the body made the lid spring up.

Yohann peered down into the darkened interior and when he couldn't see anything he felt around inside. The strongbox was empty, except for a single gold coin.

'Damn,' he said.

16

'It's been a while,' Oliver Kincaid said, 'since you last came to Dirtwood, but I don't have any information for you.'

The bounty hunter Lee Gould shoved two customers aside to get closer to the bar in the bustling saloon room.

'This time I'm the one with information,' he said. Then, when Oliver cupped an ear towards him, signifying he couldn't hear him, he raised his voice to be heard over the rowdy customers. 'I have information.'

Oliver placed a whiskey bottle on the bar and poured Lee a measure.

'Then tell me quickly. We're busy in here tonight.'

A customer barged into Lee, making him wince, while another man leaned over his shoulder to demand service.

'The Hunter's Moon was a lot

quieter the last time I came.'

'It was, but the saloon has a new name. We're the Queen of Hearts now.'

'Why the change?'

'Because a lot's happened in the last six months. The original saloon got burned down, but I took a risk. I borrowed some money and I built a bigger and better saloon. Luckily, my new bartender is a queen of hearts in all ways and she's turned out to be a good attraction.'

Oliver gestured at Wilhelmina who was adroitly serving one customer while simultaneously flirting with two more and batting away several others who were clamouring for her attention.

'In that case I may be able to help you get an even bigger draw. I have information about the man who used to enthral customers in this very saloon with lively tales about his adventures.'

Oliver drew the whiskey bottle away. 'If I had a dollar for every customer who's tried to sell me details of what happened to my brother, I could afford to open another saloon.'

Lee sipped his whiskey. 'You can't afford to ignore this story. Last month I was resting up in Prudence when I met a man in a saloon. That man told me he'd had a drink with a man who'd played poker with a man who said he'd heard about Trip getting chased out of — '

'I've heard enough already!'

Oliver cautioned Lee to stay where he was while he served Doctor Tweedmouth. When he returned, he drew him to the only quiet spot at the end of the bar.

'But you have to hear this tale,' Lee said. 'Trip used to get involved in all sorts of exploits and this story sounds like something only he could have done.'

Oliver laughed. 'Trip sure did get himself into some scrapes, but he isn't the only Kincaid who's led a colourful life and who has exciting stories to tell.'

Oliver didn't explain, but he slapped his belly, which with some pleasure he noted wasn't as substantial as once it had been, inviting Lee to look him up and down.

'You?' Lee spluttered with his eyes wide and incredulous.

'Sure.' Oliver leaned over the bar and drew Lee into a conspiratorial huddle. 'Have you heard of the legend of the dead men's gold?'

Lee snorted and jerked upright. 'If I had a dollar for every tall tale I've heard about that stash of cursed gold, I wouldn't need the gold.'

'It's the same for me, but it'll be worth a dollar to add a true story to the legend.' Oliver winked. 'I believe Trip found the gold and now he's living a new, secret life somewhere out there.'

Lee frowned sympathetically. 'It sure would be mighty fine if that had happened.'

'I reckon so too, and I believe there'll come a time when he'll decide it's safe to come out of hiding. So one day I'll be tending bar here as usual and without warning he'll come walking back in through that door, as if he'd never been away.'

Oliver looked at the door. When that made Lee glance that way, with impeccable timing a newcomer stepped into the doorway.

As the man surveyed the busy saloon, Oliver did a double take and looked him over. It took him a moment to accept that the new customer wasn't Trip, but by then Lee had noticed his reaction.

'You really believe that, don't you, that one day Trip will return?'

'One day,' Oliver said with a catch in his throat.

'In that case,' Lee said, throwing a dollar on the bar, 'tell me the true story behind the legend of the dead men's gold.'

We do hope that you have enjoyed reading this large print book.

Did you know that all of our titles are available for purchase?

We publish a wide range of high quality large print books including:
**Romances, Mysteries, Classics
General Fiction
Non Fiction and Westerns**

Special interest titles available in large print are:
**The Little Oxford Dictionary
Music Book, Song Book
Hymn Book, Service Book**

Also available from us courtesy of Oxford University Press:
**Young Readers' Dictionary
(large print edition)
Young Readers' Thesaurus
(large print edition)**

For further information or a free brochure, please contact us at:
**Ulverscroft Large Print Books Ltd.,
The Green, Bradgate Road, Anstey,
Leicester, LE7 7FU, England.
Tel:** (00 44) **0116 236 4325**
Fax: (00 44) **0116 234 0205**

INCIDENT AT
BUTLER'S STATION

Neil Hunter

For Cavalry Sergeant Ed Blaine, wounded by an Apache lance, the way station offered a chance to recover. All he wanted was a place to rest. But it was not to be . . . First he met up with the girl he had once been about to marry. Then he found himself under the guns of a bunch of outlaws waiting to free their brother from an incoming stage. Then, just when Blaine figured it couldn't get any worse, Butler's Station was hit by a band of warring Apaches . . .

NEBRASKA SHOOT-OUT

Corba Sunman

Jeff Arlen, a detective with the Butterworth Agency, is on the trail of Alec Frome, who has stolen $10,000 from the bank where he works. Riding into Sunset Ridge, Nebraska, he hopes to find Frome in the town where he'd once lived. But, soon after his arrival, he is drawn into a perilous local battle. Capturing Frome and retrieving the stolen money looks like child's play compared to what he now faces, which will only be resolved with plenty of hot lead.

LAST STAGE FROM HELL'S MOUTH

Derek Rutherford

Sam Cotton is the last person anyone in the New Mexico town of Hope would have suspected of wrongdoing. All that changes, however, when he is seen riding away hell for leather from a scene of robbery and death. Though the victims' families save him from a lynching, once the judge arrives in town, Sam will stand trial for his life — with only his father believing in his innocence . . .